THE CHILDREN OF
CROKE PARK

MICHAEL FOLEY is originally from Killavullen, County Cork. His first book, *Kings of September*, won the 2007 Boyle Sports Irish Sports Book of the Year. He also ghostwrote *Harte: Presence Is the Only Thing*, the autobiography of Tyrone Gaelic football manager Mickey Harte, shortlisted for the 2009 William Hill Irish Sports Book of the Year.

A four-time GAA McNamee Award winner, his third book, *The Bloodied Field*, won Best GAA Publication at the 2015 Awards. Michael was also shortlisted for Sports Journalist of the Year in 2003, 2013 and 2017. Michael is deputy sports editor and sportswriter for the Irish edition of the *Sunday Times*. He currently resides in Macroom, County Cork.

THE CHILDREN OF
CROKE PARK

BLOODY SUNDAY 1920

MICHAEL FOLEY

THE O'BRIEN PRESS
DUBLIN

First published 2023 by The O'Brien Press Ltd,
12 Terenure Road East, Rathgar, Dublin 6, D06 HD27, Ireland.
Tel: +353 1 4923333; Fax: +353 1 4922777
E-mail: books@obrien.ie
Website: obrien.ie
The O'Brien Press is a member of Publishing Ireland.

ISBN: 978-1-78849-384-0

7 6 5 4 3 2 1
27 26 25 24 23

Printed and bound by CPI Group (UK) Ltd, Croydon, CR0 4YY.
The paper in this book is produced using pulp from managed forests.

Published in:

**DUBLIN
UNESCO**
City of Literature

DEDICATION

To Karen, Thomas, Liam, Adam and Eoin

IRELAND IN 1920

• By 1916, Ireland had been occupied by British forces
for over 800 years, as part of a mighty empire that spread
across the globe.

• In Easter of that year, a group of Irish Volunteers took
over the General Post Office in Dublin and proclaimed a
new, independent Irish republic.

• Fierce fighting lasted for five days, ending in the sur-
render of the rebels. Their leaders were executed, drawing
huge sympathy.

• In 1917, thousands of rebels were released from prisons
in Britain and returned to Ireland. Some rejoined the Irish
Volunteers – soon to become known as the Irish Republican Army (IRA).

• On 21 January 1919, two policemen of the Royal Irish
Constabulary (RIC) were killed by an IRA ambush at
Soloheadbeg in County Tipperary, beginning the Irish War
of Independence.

- For nearly two years, the IRA fought a guerrilla war against police and the military, launching surprise attacks before disappearing back into the community.

- The police were strengthened in 1920 by two extra forces – the Black and Tans, named after the colour of their uniforms – and the Auxiliaries, a special group focused on chasing down the IRA. Both groups are still remembered in Ireland for their cruelty.

- Eventually, the British forces had the IRA under severe pressure. One of the IRA's most famous leaders, Michael Collins, wanted to strike back. He chose to target a list of suspected British spies.

- On the morning of Sunday, 21 November 1920, Collins's specially selected Squad, assisted by other IRA members, attacked a range of targets across Dublin, killing or mortally wounding fifteen people.

- The Dublin and Tipperary Gaelic football teams were due to play a match that same afternoon at Croke Park, Dublin. A huge crowd turned up, including three young boys: William, Jerome and Billy.

THE BOYS

JEROME O'LEARY is ten years old and lives on Blessington Street in Dublin with his parents and sister Mary.

WILLIAM ROBINSON is eleven years old and lives in the heart of the city, on Little Britain Street, with his parents and brother Patrick.

JOHN WILLIAM SCOTT is fourteen years old and lives with his parents, his grandfather and his brother Fred on Fitzroy Avenue. Croke Park sits right at the end of the street.

CHAPTER ONE

PERRY

My name is William Robinson, but you can call me Perry like everyone else does. I'm eleven years old and I live in the middle of Dublin city on Little Britain Street, in a room with my mother and father and my brother Patrick. Now, my story starts without me in it. I know that doesn't sound like it makes any sense. But give me a second and I'll tell you how it happened.

At least, this is how I think it happened.

There were two boys running like mad out of the fruit and vegetable market up the way from home, running like they needed to skidoo, and fast. If you know the place, the Ormond Market right in the middle of Dublin, you'll know this story is true.

This man was chasing them. He was chubby and red-faced and puffing, running out from the market, and the boys sprinting away from him. They ran down alleys and dodged around the boys and girls out playing in the street, and they barely missed falling into all the older people gathered in the doorways, talking.

The lad in front, Jimmy, was running as he fast as he could, carrying a small box of apples they had lifted from one of the traders. The lad behind was Jack, trying not to tread on the few apples that bounced out of the box onto the cobbles.

They turned down a narrow alley that was lined with horse stables and animal pens. Jimmy kicked in the door on one. It swung open. The boys dived inside and pulled the door shut.

Now, this next bit I saw myself, so I absolutely know it happened.

'Stop those fellas!' shouted the man again. His belly was jiggling beneath his dirty, white apron. He tripped over some small children and bounced off another man, twirling around like a ballerina before sliding on a patch of horse manure that sent him tumbling to the ground.

He got up, soaked in filthy water and muck. His apron was covered with pieces of wet straw. He looked like a big old stuffed scarecrow.

The man looked up the alley, but the boys had disappeared. He put his hands on his knees, trying to catch his breath. He was sweating and wheezing.

'Where are yez?!' he shouted. 'I'll find you, and when I do it's across to the police station for the pair of yez!'

Jimmy and Jack kept as still as statues. They were sitting in a pig pen, on straw that stank of dung, holding their breaths. Jimmy looked out between the cracks in the timber door after a little while. The man wasn't there, but Jimmy could still hear him shouting down the alley outside.

And again, I know this next bit happened for sure, because Jack told me himself. And whatever about Jimmy, Jack is a sound lad.

'Okay we've got fifteen apples,' Jimmy said to him. 'Seven for you, eight for me.'

'Wha'?' said Jack.

'Extra one for me because I had to carry them,' says Jimmy.

'You sure?' says Jack. 'Let me count them.'

'Look,' says Jimmy, growing impatient. 'Take the apples and go home.'

'But I can't carry them all,' Jack says. 'Where'll I hide them?'

'Oh, sweet suffering damnation,' Jimmy says, just like his da would say any time he got annoyed. 'Just put them in your pockets. Throw a few under your hat. Stick them down your trousers.'

'Down me trousers?'

'I don't care where you put them! Just stick them some place. Now, let's go.'

Jimmy eased open the door and peered out. There was no sign of the man. So he tucked five apples into his pockets, hid one in his hat and carried one in each hand.

'Right. I'll see ya,' he said, nodding at Jack.

'Yeah, see ya,' Jack replied, still stuffing the seven apples wherever he could. He struggled to the top of the alley, holding the apples in his arms, trying not to drop them.

Then he saw me. I was on my way back from my granny's on Moore Street, just up and around the corner. He looked worried.

'Robinson!' he shouted. 'Perry!'

I walked down to him, taking in the sight of this fella covered in straw and muck, carrying a load of apples.

'Where did ya get those? And uuughhhh ...'

I made a bit of a face.

'You stink worse than rotten fish! Ah, Jack, is the water bad at home?!'

Jack shook his head and scowled a little bit.

'C'mere a sec,' he said. 'Take three of those, will ya? I can't carry them all.'

'Are ya sure?' I replied. 'I'll bring them home for you if you want.'

'No, I'll only get in trouble. Just take them.'

'But what'll I tell me ma?' I said.

'Just make something up. You got them from the penny dinner house or something. I don't know.'

Then he told me the whole story in about ten seconds flat, talking non-stop: the chase, hiding in the stable and all the bits in between.

'You goin' to the match tomorrow?' he said.

'Yeah,' I replied. 'Think so. You?'

'Oh, sweet suffering damnation ...'

Jack was looking up the street. The sight of a man in the distance had made him pale.

'That's me da! Gotta run!'

And he sprinted back down the alley, slipping and sliding on the muck as he went. I stuffed two apples into my pocket and bit into the last one.

It was delicious, so sweet and fresh. The juices ran down the sides of my mouth as I turned the corner onto Little Britain Street. I weaved through the crowd of women at the front door to our tenement house and bounded up the stairs, two steps at a time.

The house was always crowded and busy. People would be out the front and around the stairs, dawdling in conversation. Children were always running up and down the steps. I bumped into an old lady on the last flight of steps before our room.

'Mother of Mercy, Perry! You'll have me killed with the speed of ya!'

'Sorry missus!' I said. I wasn't sure who it was, with the shawl covering her head, but it must have been a neighbour.

I finally reached our front door and swept in like a returning hero, placing two apples on the table.

'There ya go, Ma, a little something for your tea.'

My mother stared hard. 'Where did these come from?'

'Jack from school gave me them. He had loads.'

'And where did Jack get them?'

I shrugged. 'Sure, I don't know. The market I suppose.'

We both turned as the door opened and slammed shut. It was my father.

'Patrick,' said my mother. 'He's come home with a load of apples. We're not rearing a thief!'

My face turned red.

'I'm not a thief!' I said. 'Jack just gave them to me.'

My father gazed down at the two bright green apples sitting on the table.

'Listen to your mother, Perry,' he said, picking an apple up, rubbing it against his shirt and taking a gigantic bite. 'But I suppose if we don't eat them, someone else will.'

CHAPTER TWO

My da wiped away the juice with his sleeve as it dribbled down his cheek. He was smiling. Sure, how couldn't you? They were gorgeous. Then he looked at me and frowned.

'Stay out of the markets unless you're in there with me. Here, Bridget.'

He tossed the other apple into the air for my ma to catch before he flopped down on our old, faded armchair. She caught the apple and frowned at him. I frowned as well. Da said things like that a lot.

'Stay out of the streets after dark unless you're there with me.'

'Come straight home from school unless you're looking for me.'

'Stay out of the pubs unless you're trying to find me.'

I knew why he said those things – around our way wasn't the safest spot. But I loved the feel of the streets outside when I was on my own.

I lived in the Ormond Slum. There was a time when these crumbling old buildings were homes to the finest families of Dublin. But when the rich people all moved out to the countryside, the houses filled up with the likes of us, the poor of the city.

Families lived in small, single rooms like ours, sharing toilets and taps with their neighbours. The place smelled of damp and decay. You'd trip over the rats in the rubbish around the place, nibbling on scraps and getting fat. The smoke of fires lit to keep the houses warm mixed with the smell of animal manure from the streets outside.

All of the men here worked in the fruit market. Loads of the women sold fish on stalls around the city. My da worked as a carter, driving a horse and cart, carrying whatever people needed him to move. Everyone wheeled and dealed, gathering boxes of anything, buying and selling goods around the tenements for almost nothing, because that's all anyone could afford.

We didn't have much, but we made our fun. We made footballs from old socks and paper. Old boxes got remade into dolls' houses. We played Tans and Shinners around the streets like other children played Cowboys and Indians. Tans were like the police, the lads over from England terrorising everyone. The Shinners were the IRA, the rebels they were chasing.

We collected old jam jars and stout bottles to sell for scrap. We gathered any old food and sold it to the pig raisers. Some lads pitched pennies and played cards.

The handball players played their games in the concrete alley beside Halston Street prison. The rubber ball made a nice popping sound when it bounced against the wall, and again when a player made clean contact with the palm of his hand. My da loved playing, and I loved watching him.

All sorts lived here. There was old soldiers without a penny, using their army overcoats for blankets, and fellas who told their stories about fighting in the Rebellion in 1916. At night, you could hear songs on the street, as fellas came out of the pubs – songs about rebels and fighting with the police.

You'd hear glass smashing and the odd gunshot. More than the odd one sometimes.

I could see why me da would say to be careful where you go and what you're at. But I was never at much. Sure, eating the odd stolen apple wouldn't kill a fella.

'Are you going to match tomorrow, Dad?' I asked.

'Ach, I don't know,' he replied. 'Dublin, Tipperary. The crowds – there'll be a silly lot up from the country. And a day at the match isn't cheap, you know. Is the weather to be good tomorrow? There's better ways to spend a sunny Sunday than at Croke Park, isn't there, Bridget?'

He smiled and stood up, gathering my mother into his arms and dancing her across the floor, humming a tune. You'd be mortified at them.

'Patrick, you old hack, will you stop!' cried my ma, unable to keep from laughing. He let her go, bowing like she was a queen, then looked back across at me.

'But you go up if you want to, Perry. You have your spot, don't ya?'

I nodded. I knew where he meant. Just over the bridge crossing the canal at the corner of Croke Park stood a big tree, on the bank that ran along behind the goals. I knew the nice crook up there he was thinking of. From up in that tree, high above the crowd below, you could see the whole field.

'And there'll be no leaves on the trees either in November,' he said. 'Best spot in the house, lad.'

'Yeah, I think so,' I said. 'I'll probably go.'

'Good lad,' my father said. 'And shout plenty. Dublin need all the help they can get.'

'What? No way! They're gonna win,' I replied. 'There's no way they'll lose to that Tipperary crowd.'

'Ah, Perry, it's as easy catch ya!' he smiled back.

Then he bent down and whispered in my ear.

'And thanks for the apple.'

CHAPTER THREE

That Saturday night before the match was one of those noisy, lively nights on the street outside. If you only heard the roaring and screeching, at whatever time it was. There was fellas fighting and women shouting at them. And I swore I heard a gun. I was worn out listening to it, trying to sleep.

I was lying still, frozen under the covers beside Patrick, the brother. The fire was nearly out and the only light was creeping in around the edges of the curtain from the street lamp outside. I jiggled my feet around to try to warm up the sheets, but all I got was groans from yer man and a kick in the knee.

It's funny how scary things can get into your head when it gets past the time you'd normally be asleep. All sorts of stuff was running through my brain.

I started thinking about my granny on Moore Street. She often told me stories about living there through the Rising in 1916. The fighting was going on right across the road in the GPO, the big post office on Sackville Street. The British army bombed it till the people inside couldn't take any more. The fire and the flames were so hot, granny could feel the heat way down across the street.

People brought buckets of water across to kill the flames. They thought the rebels inside were being burned alive. But then the firing got so bad everyone just stayed back, inside their own houses.

They stayed inside saying prayers, hiding. Waiting for it to be over.

Life was hard where we lived, but you never felt you were in danger. I never did anyway. The neighbours were all good people, and we all looked after each other. My ma often said everyone in our building reared each other. We were all in this life together, like. It was a nice thing to say. It was a nice feeling to know people were looking out for you.

But bad things happened. Bad things do, no matter how many good people are around. Every house had its stories, sad ones. I'll tell you about my Uncle William, because he's an interesting one. And I'll tell you later about my cousin Sam, because he's another interesting one.

Both of them are interesting for kind of the same reasons, but then they're totally different.

But they're nearly the same, if you get me?

And they're related, even though they're so different in ways. Which I suppose doesn't really matter. Lots of people in families are different, but they still love each other and look after each other.

Right?

I'm talking too much.

I'll tell you about Uncle William.

He lived just up the street in another tenement building, with my auntie Christina and my four cousins, Mary, Bernard, Thomas and William junior.

He had been a British soldier during the First World War and played soccer for Jacob's FC. Jacob's was a big biscuit factory on the other side of the River Liffey, the river that splits Dublin in two. I often imagined that a biscuit factory must be a magical place, with big chimneys belching out smoke while the inside would be all warm and cosy from the heat of the ovens, baking hundreds of biscuits and cakes.

Actually, don't mind the hundreds. It must have been thousands.

But the way William told it, Jacob's wasn't like that at all. It was a hard, cruel place to work. They called the soccer team The Red Necks, for the way the big bags of biscuit flour scraped and scratched against the men's necks when they carried them.

I remember something William said once about working there. He recalled what a union man named Jim Larkin once said of the place – that working in Jacob's was like sending those men from this Earth twenty years before their time.

The Jacob's soccer team played their games at a pitch on Rutland Avenue in Crumlin, on the edge of the city. It wasn't far from us really, but it was like another world out there in the country. Olympia were their big rivals, and they played out near Mount Jerome cemetery, not far from Crumlin, heading for Harold's Cross. Their ground was up on the side of a hill.

'The pitch is so lopsided,' my father told me once, 'the fella playing on the left wing can barely see the lad on the right wing below him.'

And were they rivals? Ah, it was bitter stuff. They were all working men, and when you think about it, they were all the same in lots of ways. But other things can get in the way, dividing people for no great reason.

Jacob's gladly welcomed British soldiers like Uncle William onto their team. Olympia didn't. Olympia included a few players that everyone knew were in the IRA.

When Jacob's played Olympia, people were always interested, because the matches often got cranky. The last time they played was this year, in the spring. It ended as a scoreless draw, but no one cared about the result afterwards.

From what William told us, the Olympia players had taunted the Jacob's lads all through the game for having soldiers on their team. Then the Jacob's players invaded the Olympia dressing rooms after the match, looking for a fight.

William laughed telling that, Because you would, wouldn't you? The Red Necks taking on the Shinners. Gas stuff.

But it got a bit serious afterwards. When the people who ran the League tried to figure out what had happened, most of the Jacob's players refused to tell their side of the story. They said they were afraid of the Olympia lads coming after them again. They were nearly afraid of their lives, William said.

But that stuff never bothered William. A few players got barred from playing a few games and that was it. The way William told it, the Ormond was our place.

'We were born here,' he said.

'We play here.

'We work here.

'Some of us even fought here.'

And he really believed that, right up to the end. On a night that October, Uncle William was out near home with three friends when two men stopped them. What happened next? Well, Da kept the bit that appeared in the paper the following day. Here it is:

MYSTERIOUS AFFAIR
Young Man Shot Last Night

A sensational shooting affair occurred in Little Mary Street at 11.45 o'clock last night, as a result of which William Robinson, an ex-soldier, lies in a critical condition.

The story of the affair related to an Evening Herald representative by one of those on the scene was that Robinson, who is an ex-soldier, and three or four others were standing at the corner of Capel Street and Mary Street when two men in civilian attire approached them. One of them wore a black velour hat, a navy blue suit and a soft collar and who, speaking with an Irish accent, conducted the entire conversation which followed, addressed one of the group, asking what he was doing there at that hour of the night. 'I replied,' said our informant, 'that we were having a chat and it was not 12 o'clock yet.

He then asked, 'Are you Sinn Féiners?' and I said, 'Why do you ask that?' 'Because,' he said, 'we are Republican Police.' 'Even if you are,' I asked, 'what do want to know that for?'

'He then asked for proof in writing that this young man was a Sinn Féiner, to which he replied, 'Supposing I am, why should I show you proof of it?' Robinson then asked, 'What proof do you want?' then jokingly added, 'Come across the road and I will show you proof in writing.'

The two strangers, Robinson, and one or two of the others, then crossed the road to a dark spot in Little Mary Street. One of the party, according to this account, told Robinson not to go down there, and the next thing he observed was the strangers drawing two revolvers. One of them, who was in front, said, 'Fire,' and they fired about three shots each.

Robinson ran back, and just as he got round the corner he fell and said, 'I am wounded.' Two of the party then followed the strangers down East Arran Street and Pill Lane, shouting, 'Stop those two,' losing sight of them near the Bridewell.

They then returned and carried the wounded man to Jervis St Hospital.

They state that a bullet went through his ankle and another lodged in his stomach. His condition appeared to be critical and he was suffering a lot of pain, though quite conscious. He was attended by Rev Fr Sheehan, Pro-Cathedral. A bullet passed between the legs of another of the party, cutting his trousers and grazing his shin.

The second 'mystery man', it is stated, did not speak at all and appeared to be trying to keep his face away from the group.

Robinson is a well-known member of the Jacob football team and resided at Stafford Street.

The Republican Police were set up by Sinn Féin to police the areas where they were strong. Uncle William died at nine o'clock that night. People said such tragedy had rarely been seen on the street. A few days later, we all gathered for the funeral at the church across the square from our tenement.

Ah, that day was just too sad. My cousins were all gathered around my auntie Christina. Mary had just turned six. Bernard was four and Thomas three. William junior was a year old. I could barely breathe at times for trying to hold back the tears, thinking of them and imagining what it would be like if the same thing happened to my ma or da.

And now I was in bed in the middle of the night, with the sounds of the street and the whistles of the police and the drunks roaring their heads off keeping me awake, and I was thinking of Uncle William. I can still see his face in the picture in the paper that following day. He was wearing his football shirt. He looked strong and proud.

I'd say he'd have liked that, getting his picture in the paper in his Jacob's shirt. That's how I remember him anyway, doing his thing. Doing it his way.

'We're proud of him,' my da said at the funeral.

We were. And I know I said I'd tell you about Sam too, but we'll come back to Sam in a while. Right now, in this story, it's time I went to sleep.

CHAPTER FOUR

JERRY

Late on Saturday night, Jerry O'Leary lay in bed under his covers. The dull, muffled sound of voices drifted through the walls. He turned his head sideways and strained to hear the words.

'Where are you going at this time of night?'

'Out. For work.'

'Where?'

'Just out! Look, you don't need to know, so don't ask me.'

'But Jerome, what if something happens and I need to find you? How would I know where to start?'

'Nothing's going to happen.'

'But it might!'

'But it won't.'

Jerry heard the door slam shut. These conversations sometimes seeped under his bedroom door at night like smoke. Jerry didn't like them. He didn't understand them. His mother sounded worried. His dad sounded agitated. Not at each other; it didn't feel like an argument. But it made his tummy quiver a lot.

Moonlight seeped in around the fringes of the curtains.

The night sky outside was clear, without a fleck of cloud. The warmth of the fire downstairs was dissolving and his room was getting cold. Jerry felt the chill on his nose and pulled the covers up to his eyes. Eventually, he disappeared underneath under the blankets altogether.

His house was in the middle of Dublin, on Blessington Street. Mrs Curran and her family lived downstairs. Jerry, his sister Mary and his parents shared two rooms – one for sleeping, one for everything else. Every night, Jerry could hear the click of footsteps on the street outside and murmurs of conversation as people walked past the front door.

Sometimes when they were alone in the house like this, he stayed awake and listened to see if his mother was asleep. He might creep onto the landing and wait for the rattle and clunk of the front door opening, the gentle high-pitched squeal of the hinge and his father's steps ascending the stairs. Mary sometimes groaned from the depths of her slumber.

'Jer … where are you … what are you …'

'Sshhh! Quiet, you!'

Jerry tried to start a dream that might take him to sleep. The following day promised adventure. All week in school, the boys had talked about the Gaelic football game in Croke Park. Tipperary were coming to play Dublin. It wasn't an All-Ireland final; there wasn't any kind of trophy involved at all.

But all the fighting meant the authorities had stopped all of these matches, so this one meant a lot.

Jerry was from Dublin, so Dublin was his team. It was the same for the Tipperary people, or the Cork people, or the Galway crowd. Wherever you were from, that was the team you followed.

And Dublin were good, even if he often heard his father and others say they should be an awful lot better. He didn't mind. They were Jerry's heroes.

He ran the names through his head: Johnny McDonnell in goals – the Man in the Cap, they called, him for the way he always wore his cap when he played. Then there were the Synnott brothers, who lived down near the city docks, not far from where Jerome lived.

Frank Burke had fought in the Rebellion a few years before, in 1916. Everyone knew Frank's story: how he had been taught in school by Patrick Pearse, the rebel leader; how he went to prison, but came back and played hurling with Dublin in 1917. He even won an All-Ireland medal that year.

As a footballer, Frank Burke was like electricity, but Jerome often thought about Paddy McDonnell as the spark that lit up the whole team. Paddy was another star, a tall, beanpole of a player at centre field. Johnny the goalkeeper was his brother. Paddy was also Dublin's captain and their inspiration.

Jerry's father talked of Paddy the same way as Jerry. Without Paddy to catch the ball and kick it to Frank Burke, he'd say, would Frank Burke ever get the ball in the first place? How good would Frank Burke and all the rest be without Paddy McDonnell? That made a lot of sense to Jerry.

The bedroom was getting colder. Jerry curled up tighter beneath the covers. He imagined playing for Dublin the following day, wearing the bright blue jersey and dark navy shorts. He was in the dressing room, listening to the captain gather them all together with his final words. Jerry remembered again the headlines in his father's newspaper:

GAA Challenge Match
Tipperary (challengers) v Dublin
(Leinster champions)
An All-Ireland test
At Croke Park tomorrow, 21 November, at 2.45pm
A thrilling game expected!

Jerry sits now in the dressing room of his imagination, his legs bouncing with nerves. He isn't ten years old here, but a grown man, making real his dreams.

He imagines Paddy McDonnell standing in front of them all, his huge fist clenched till his knuckles turn white.

'Leave nothing behind us in this room, lads. Nothing! Give everything out on that field!'

He feels the closeness as the players squeeze out through the dressing room door. The noise of the crowd sweeps down from the main stand behind him, warming the back of his neck on a freezing cold day.

The scene jumps ahead. Jerry leaps to catch a ball. He runs past Tipperary men, making little side-steps like Frank Burke might. He accelerates forward. The Tipperary goalkeeper is crouched in goal, ready. Jerry gathers himself and fires a searing shot at goal.

He feels that perfect contact of the ball against his boot. The action freezes like a picture in his head. He rolls the image back and forth in his mind, the ball rocketing past the goalkeeper to the top corner of the net every time.

The crowd roars. Jerry smiles and salutes them. His team-mates carry him off the field shoulder-high, as the crowd roars and newspaper men rush up, trying to get a word with the hero O'Leary.

He opened his eyes again. Still awake. Jerry turned in the bed, almost kicking the blankets away in frustration.

A still-sleeping voice said, 'Jerry … would ya stop?'

Mary. Annoying Mary.

Sometimes Jerry wondered if his father might be a spy, passing information in the dead of night. That's what some people said. He heard them saying it, and all because he worked in the Castle. He was in and out of there every day. Jerry's father was an accountant. He worked with numbers, helping mind every penny spent by the British in Ireland.

'It's that simple,' his father once told him. 'People make assumptions. But the same people don't always know the truth.'

The night dragged on. Minutes passed like hours. Jerry watched the shadow visible under the door in the hallway outside, as his mother moved around in the other room, tidying and cleaning.

There was a tinkle of a bell on the street, like the bell on the trucks that carried Black and Tans and Auxiliary police around the city at night. Jerry tiptoed across the floor and pulled back the curtain a little. A light was coming from a house across the road. Police were crowding around the front door, shouting.

'Alright! Open up! Open up this blasted door or we're kicking it in!'

A couple of Auxiliaries stood on the street outside as the rest piled into the hall. He watched an Auxiliary looking across the road at the upper floors of the houses on Jerry's side. He seemed to linger on Jerry's window. Had he seen him?

Jerry pulled his head back and closed the curtains. What had he done? What would happen now? He heard screaming from across the street. There was the sound of something breaking, like a window or a vase. Then the same voice as before, shouting again.

'Let's go, lads! Nothing here but pale boys and old women.'

The engine of the truck started up. Jerry slid the curtain back just enough to peek out with one eye. The Auxiliaries were gone.

He slumped back into bed, still gathering his breath. The street was silent again. A few minutes later, he heard his own front door clunk open and gently click shut, his father padding up the stairs.

There was muffled conversation in the other room. His mother made tea. They drank a cup, then the glimmer of light seeping through the bottom of the door disappeared. Jerry shut his eyes and pretended to be asleep as his mother and father slid into their bed. His father was home and safe. Mary hadn't stirred once. Everyone now surrendered to peaceful sleep.

CHAPTER FIVE

There wasn't another sound until Jerry heard the sizzle of cooking on the stove. Sunday morning meant sausages and bacon. That was enough to bounce him out of bed.

He walked across the room and pulled back the curtains. The room filled with sunlight so bright it made him squint.

He looked out the window and across the street to where he had watched the Auxiliaries the night before. There was nobody there now. The street was quiet, save for a few people making their way here and there. He heard boys shouting the newspaper headlines from the street corners of the city. The newspaper boys are out, he thought. It must be late.

He quickly put on his clothes and bounded down the stairs at top speed.

'Good Lord in Heaven, Jerry,' his mother cried. 'We heard you before we saw you. Sit down and eat.'

He looked at the clock. It was after 9.30am.

'We don't have much time,' she said. 'We're off to Mass soon, so hurry on.'

Jerry looked across the table at his sister Mary. She was staring at him. Mary was thirteen, three years older than Jerry. Sometimes he reckoned Mary thought she was the boss of the house, always with their mother in the kitchen and talking like they were best friends, then talking to him like she was his mother.

'You're not the boss!' he'd tell her.

But sometimes she did kind things. One day, when his writing for school was a bit messy, she came and fixed it before anyone else got to see it. She made his 'i' look less like an 'l' and put a couple of tails on any 'a' that was turning into an 'o'. She might share any spare cake at the bottom of a box. Small things like that, like a friend would do. She was good that way.

This morning, though, her stare was hard and cross. Jerry munched down on another bit of sausage and stared back.

'What?'

Mary's eyes narrowed and she began speaking slowly and quietly in a way that threatened trouble.

'Can you just. Stop. Chewing. Like. THAT!'

'Like what?' asked Jerry, tearing off a bigger chunk of sausage and chewing now with his mouth wide open.

'Like that!'

'Mary.'

Their mother was at the sink wiping clean the frying pan. She turned around and looked at the two of them.

'That's enough. Jerry, don't be bothering her.'

'But I'm not,' he replied. 'I'm just eating these deeeeeeeeee-liciousss sausages.'

He took another bite and chewed again with his mouth open. Little chunks of sausage fell from his mouth.

'Mmmmm. So tasty.'

This was all too much for Mary.

'Quit it! Ma, it's like he's eating carrots. You rotten donkey!'

Jerry threw his head back with laughter.

'Hee-haw! Hee-haw!' he howled.

'Jerry! Mary!' his mother shouted. 'That's enough, the pair of you! Jerry, those boots are all scuffed. Did you not clean them yesterday? Get some polish and shine them up before Mass. Mary, come here and make a pot of tea before we go.'

Mary ate the last piece of bacon on her plate, still scowling at her brother. Jerry skipped across the room, the butt of his last sausage hanging from his mouth like a cigar. His father was sitting in the corner in his armchair, trying to mend a broken picture frame on his lap.

'Jerry, what are you at?" he said, without looking up from the frame. 'God love us, there's enough racket in the house without you making any more.'

Jerry took a moment to listen and couldn't hear a sound in the house, but he knew what his father meant and he wasn't about to answer back. His father liked the house quiet and orderly and neatly balanced, like a perfectly tallied sum.

Some evenings, his father told the children parts of his story. He was from Cork, at entirely the other end of the country to Dublin. He had moved up to Limerick city as a young man and found a job as a clerk and bookkeeper with the local Council. Then he met Mary Jane.

'Imagine!' he often said, 'we both came all the way from Cork to meet in Limerick and finish up with you two in Dublin.'

They married and settled first in Limerick, where Mary was born. 'Mary Angela, to be precise,' her mother would say. Two years later, in 1908, their first boy was born. He was called John, but he died when he was a baby. Their little angel brother, Jerry and Mary were always told, watching over them all.

'Then you came along, Jerry,' his father would say. 'We called you after me, Jerome.'

'Which has caused no end of confusion since,' his mother often said. He always remembered her telling that part.

'Jerome, Jerry, Jeremiah … We should have called you Patrick or Sean or Augustine!'

'Augustine?!' roared Jerry.

'Well, you'd know I was calling you then!' said his mother, stifling the laughter.

'So, are you going to the match later?' his father asked him.

'Oh, I think so, Da,' Jerry replied.

'By yourself?' asked his father, pushing together two corners of the broken picture frame carefully but firmly.

'Yeah, but I might l meet some of the boys on the way,' Jerry said.

'Because,' his father replied, reaching for a cloth to wipe some extra glue from the corner of the frame, 'I was going to go myself. What do you think?'

Jerry's heart jumped a little. He didn't mind going by himself, but he loved going with his dad.

The routine was always the same. They would leave Blessington Street and walk up towards Croke Park. His father would take a scoop of tobacco from his pouch and fill his pipe, crack a match to light the tobacco and start puffing away.

They would stop at the shop on the corner and buy chocolate bars – smooth, milky chocolate bars. If Jerome ever lit up at home, the smell of pipe smoke always made Jerry's tummy rumble. It was like the aroma went together in his head with chocolate. The taste of chocolate always made Jerry think of matches with his dad.

But he didn't want to appear too pushed. After all, heading off to Croke Park by himself was the sort of freedom any ten-year-old liked – finding his own way, bobbing along in a river of grown-ups. He wouldn't want anyone thinking he couldn't do this stuff by himself.

'Ah yeah, if you like,' Jerry said, casually.

His dad looked up, acting surprised at the tone of Jerry's voice.

'Well, I can always stay at home I suppose.'

'No,' Jerry answered quickly, then paused. 'No. Do come. It'll be a great match.'

'Right so,' his dad said. 'There. Job done.'

The frame was fixed. He turned the picture around and looked at the image. It was Jerry, sitting for a photograph the year before, in his white shirt, his brown hair nicely cropped.

'And you thought we'd broken you,' smiled his father. 'Back up on the wall now. Pride of place. I don't suppose we'll ever find out how it got broken?'

The moment the previous week when Jerry lost control of a small bouncing ball that rebounded against the wall and sent the frame crashing to the floor flashed through his head. He got such a fright he hadn't even found the ball afterwards.

'I suppose not,' he said. 'Probably Mary clomping around so hard the picture fell.'

'Hey!' shouted Mary from the sink. 'I don't clomp and it wasn't me!'

His dad looked at Jerry in a way that made him think something more was coming. Then he bent down and reached into the narrow gap between the wall and the wooden writing desk underneath the pictures.

'Nothing to do with this, so,' he said, handing the ball to Jerry.

Jerry's cheeks began to turn red. 'Dad, I …'

His dad placed a hand gently on his head.

'Sshhh. Say nothing. The polish is in the box in the cupboard beneath the sink. Shine up those shoes and we'll go to Mass.'

'Thanks, Dad,' Jerry smiled.

CHAPTER SIX

Jerry's mother was in the bedroom, making the beds and opening windows to let some fresh air in. His dad heard the shout.

'Jerome!'

'What?' they answered together. His dad smiled. Jerry's mother appeared at the doorway.

'You,' she said, pointing at Jerry. 'Polish! And as for you, is that picture fixed? Are you ready for Mass?'

'It is and I am,' Jerome said.

'Right then,' she replied. She looked at Jerry again. 'Get polishing. Time is ticking on.'

They were ready inside fifteen minutes, thundering down the stairs. Mrs Curran stood at the door of her living room, watching them.

'Good morning, O'Learys,' she smiled.

'Good morning, Mrs Curran,' replied Jerry's dad. 'A grand bright morning.'

'Sure, it's like summer out there, Mr O'Leary,' she said. 'And ye're all dressed for Mass. The Canon will be mightily impressed.'

Jerry's dad wore his suit and a grey trench coat with his dark,

42

brimmed hat. Ma had her green dress on and a light, powder-blue overcoat with a green scarf. Mary wore her purple, velvet crush dress, with white socks pulled up to her knees and her brown woollen coat.

Jerry's mother put his heavy black winter coat over his shoulders, even though the sun was shining outside. 'Well, you won't catch cold in that anyway, Jerry,' said Mrs Curran. 'It's like you're wearing a bear!'

Jerry's mother smiled. 'It's the time of year, isn't it, Mrs Curran? Can't be too careful of coughs and colds.'

'It is surely,' she agreed. 'Well, I'd best get back to this crowd in here. Have a fine morning.'

'Thank you, Mrs Curran,' they all replied as they bundled out the front door. Stepping onto the street, Jerry felt like an Arctic explorer swaddled in blankets.

'Can I not leave my coat at home?' he pleaded.

'Leave it on. That's how you catch a cold at this time of year,' his mother said. But she could feel the unseasonable heat as well.

'Open the buttons then. But leave it on you.'

They walked to St Joseph's church, a few minutes away on Berkeley Street. The church, tall and grey, was topped with sharp spires, piercing the blue morning sky. The ceiling inside reached up to the Heavens, supported by thick columns of stone, coated up to halfway in ruby-red marble.

Canon Downing was the parish priest and a well-known man throughout the city. Jerry had often heard the story about Canon Downing being listed among those lost at sea when the *HMS Leinster* was sunk by a German submarine in 1918, while sailing from Dublin to Holyhead in Wales. He had then appeared, unharmed, in the city the following day.

'The unsinkable Canon,' his dad would say with a twinkle in his eye.

The Canon also seemed unafraid to say things about events in Dublin that made most people nervous. Almost exactly two months before, the IRA had ambushed a British Army patrol in the city as they were collecting bread from a bakery. Three soldiers were killed, but when the firing stopped, the surviving soldiers pulled an eighteen-year-old boy named Kevin Barry from beneath the truck.

He was tried, sentenced to death and hanged, despite protests and pleas and prayers. The Sunday after Barry was killed, Canon Downing spoke from his own pulpit.

'I have not found in the lives of the saints anything more beautiful and more edifying than his heroic death, and resignation and tender piety in death,' he told the congregation.

It was hard to figure out who was good and bad in the city sometimes. Jerry's dad had once been a soldier in the British Army, a quartermaster sergeant with the Royal Dublin Fusiliers. 'I worked in the stores,' he told Jerry once.

'I organised supplies and made sure every soldier had what they needed.'

'Did you go to war?'

'No,' he said. 'I was never sent to the front. At the time, part of me wanted to see action, to be part of the fight. But then I saw men I knew as friends brought home from France. Whether it was by their wounds or in their minds, they were broken, Jerry. So many of them broken.' At times like that, Jerry knew not to ask any more questions.

The church was almost full when they arrived. Jerry sniffled, and his mother rummaged in her handbag.

'Here,' she whispered, passing a handkerchief along the line past Mary and his father. 'Blow your nose. I told you about the cold!' Jerry didn't sniffle again.

When Mass was over, everyone filed out of the church, the warmth of the day wrapping around them all. The O'Learys walked home, Jerome's mind drifting away to the afternoon and the trip to Croke Park.

'Who will you shout for today, Dad?'

Jerome put on a quizzical look. 'Between Dublin and Tipperary?' He pursed his lips. 'That's a hard question for a Cork man. We never want to see Tipperary go too well, but Dublin? God help us, we don't want to see Dublin getting far ahead of themselves either. Is there any way they can both lose?'

'No, Dad!'

'Well, I'll hope for a draw so,' he smiled.

Mary and her mother reached the front door first. They went inside and upstairs. Her mother had already left potatoes out to start preparing for dinner. Mary returned to the tea she had started on before they left.

She took some brown bread from the cupboard and cut four slices, placed them on four plates with knives and put the butter on the table. When the kettle was boiled she filled the teapot with hot water and added the tea leaves, then got a jug of milk.

'It's ready!' she called.

All four of them sat around the table.

'Any jam?' asked Jerry. Mary glared at him again.

There was a knock on the door. It was Mrs Curran. 'Someone for you, Mr O'Leary,' she said.

Jerome went to see who was there. Barely a minute passed before they heard the front door clanking shut. Jerome returned to the kitchen. He looked pale and gestured to his wife.

'Mary, come out here a second.'

Ma stood up and followed him to the bedroom, pulling the door closed behind her. Mary and Jerry looked at each other in bemusement. Jerry got up and went to the door.

'What are you doing?' hissed Mary.

'Ssshhh!!! I'm trying to listen.'

Jerry had his ear pressed to the bedroom door. He heard enough to stitch the story together.

'There's been attacks … IRA probably … they've killed men everywhere …'

'What'll we do?' he heard his mother say.

'Nothing at all,' Jerry's dad replied. 'This has nothing to do with us.'

His mother said something, but it was barely a whisper. Then, however, Jerry heard his father's voice so clearly that he could have been standing next to him.

'But I have to go,' he said. 'I've been summoned to the Castle.'

Jerry's head dropped. All thoughts of a day lifted by football and chocolate fragranced with pipe smoke dissolved in that moment. He knew what this meant. His dad wouldn't be home. The Castle had him now.

CHAPTER SEVEN

BILLY

The sun was shining that morning. It shone down as people gathered for Mass, glinting against the domes and the sloping roofs of the churches and cathedrals. It glittered like flecks of gold on the canal waters where young boys and men cast out fishing lines.

The sun lit up the darkest alleys, the narrow streets of the city where the poorest of the poor were huddled. It shone down on the neat row of redbrick houses on Fitzroy Avenue where John William Scott was sitting upright on his bed, reading.

The book was *Treasure Island*. Blind Pew was entering the Admiral Benbow inn, looking for the pirate Billy Bones. When he finally confronted him, Pew pressed a scrap of paper into his hand. The paper bore the dreaded black spot, the pirate code for imminent death. It meant that men were coming intent on doing harm to old Billy Bones, that his time was nigh.

John William pushed his glasses up from the edge of his nose. Thoughts drifted through his mind of Jim Hawkins, the boy caring for his mother and this inn, feeding Billy Bones rum and now faced with the wretched evil of Blind Pew. He loved stories like this, where the boy was destined to become the hero of a grand adventure. He imagined Jim Hawkins wasn't much older than him, having wild times on the high seas. That excitement must be the finest stuff of life, he thought.

He suddenly heard a voice downstairs, his father's voice.

'Billy! Billy!'

John William's father was also called John, so his mother and father always called him Billy. He bounced down onto the floor of his bedroom and lolloped downstairs. His father was sitting at the kitchen table, smiling.

'Billy, I have a joke for you.'

'You called me down here to tell me a joke?'

Billy looked at his mother tidying away plates and cutlery from breakfast time. She rolled her eyes.

'Well, no one else is laughing at it,' his father replied in a jolly way. 'I thought I'd try it out on you.'

Billy sighed. His father always had a joke, each one usually worse than the last.

'Alright, let's go.'

His father sat up in his chair and cleared his throat.

'So, a priest was quite ill, having eaten several bites of mince pie. Another priest visited him and asked if he was afraid to die.'

'From eating a mince pie?!' Billy blurted out.

'No! Wait! Just wait for the punchline!' said his father.

'Alright, sorry,' sighed Billy again.

'So the sick priest says, "No,"' continued his father, '"but I would be ashamed to die, from eating too much pie!"'

He pushed his chair back from the table, threw back his head and laughed.

'You see? Pie?! Die?!'

For a moment, Billy looked uncertainly at his mother. Should he laugh or groan? He smirked.

'Ah, Da,' he said. 'One of these days you'll find a funny one in the paper.'

'The cheek of you!' said his father, putting on a forlorn face. 'That's what you said, Mary! I get no support in this house! Not a bit!'

'I don't know where you find them,' Billy's ma replied. 'They're older than the hills, some of those jokes.'

'And they've only lasted that long because they're that funny,' he replied. 'You've no sense of humour at all.'

'And you've no sense!' said Billy as he headed out the kitchen door.

'Come back here, ya tyke!' his father shouted playfully. 'They're going in early this morning below the road.'

'Is there another game on?' Billy asked.

'Let me check,' his father replied, picking up the newspaper where he had found the joke, scanning the pages for sports articles.

'Ah, here it is. Dublin and Tipperary will be preceded by the replayed Dublin intermediate football final …'

His voice trailed off as he read to himself in silence. Billy was still looking at him.

'Who's playing?' said Billy.

'What's that? Oh yes. Erins Hope and Dunleary Commercials. Nothing much to see there, I'd have thought.'

He fixed Billy with a stare.

'You're not going over, are you?'

Billy shook his head.

'No, I have to wait for Charlie Daly. He's coming here later, then we're going over.'

'Just as well,' his father replied. 'You'd be frozen across there without your dinner, watching football matches for five hours.'

'No, we'll go in for Dublin,' Billy said. 'That'll do.'

He walked to the hall and looked out the window onto the street. Sure enough, a stream of people was already trickling down towards Croke Park at the bottom of the road.

Croke Park was both Billy's palace of dreams and his playground. Kick a ball hard enough from the front door of number 15 and it might almost make it to the gates to the field.

'If you don't end up playing for Dublin when you're that near to the place, who ever will?' the boys in school would say to him. Billy always shrugged and smiled.

It was easy enough to sneak in when the games weren't on, that much was true. Some days, he slipped in as the crowds were leaving and had a kick around. On other days, they could sidle in through the main gates if they were open, or across the flat no man's land alongside the mound people called Hill 60 and through a gap in the fence that surrounded the ground.

Sometimes Billy got a chase off the pitch from someone cutting the grass or collecting rubbish around the banks. Most times they were left alone. Those fellas were usually happy enough to see children playing football.

'Sure, that's what the place is for,' a man once said to Billy as he gathered bits of paper and discarded fruit from the pavilion stand after one game.

And so it was this Sunday. Billy and Charlie Daly would go to see Dublin playing Tipperary with half a mind on a kick about afterwards. Billy watched the crowd getting bigger along the street outside. Without thinking, he slipped out the door and took a walk down towards Croke Park.

The ticket sellers were arranging their tables. The fruit sellers were lugging their baskets down the streets, brimming with apples and oranges. Billy saw the footballers of Erins Hope and Dunleary Commercials heading in the gate, their supporters wearing wide-brimmed hats and Sunday suits.

The sun was lighting every part of the street, seeping down through the tight web of streets and alleys around Croke Park.

Billy felt a flutter in his tummy. This day promised to be special.

He heard a familiar voice again, calling his name. 'Billy! Billy!'

He looked back up the street towards his own front door. His father's head was sticking out.

'Get back up here! I thought you said you were waiting! You're going nowhere without your dinner!'

Billy wasn't planning on going down to Croke Park, not yet. Why did he find himself halfway down the street, drawn to the sports field without explanation?

Maybe part of him wanted to feel the power of being by himself, striding towards something exciting and unknown. Charlie would be down in a while and they would head off on their afternoon voyage, like Jim Hawkins, lost to adventure on the high seas.

This was their day. Croke Park was their place.

Billy turned and headed back home. Before all that, he still had to eat his dinner.

CHAPTER EIGHT

November, 1982

The old man picked up the microphone and stared at the black foam cover on top.

'So I talk into this part?'

The girl smiled. 'No, you're fine. We'll just leave it there on the table. It'll pick up everything you say.'

It was a week since the old man had received the phone call. The girl was the granddaughter of a neighbour, doing a project for university. She wanted a job in radio or television or something like that. Was this for the papers? the old man had asked.

'No, just a college project at the moment,' she said. 'But I'd love to hear your story if you wouldn't mind telling me?'

Of course, he agreed. It was years since anyone had listened to his story, or even asked.

'So, can you just say your name for the tape, and your age please?'

The old man cleared his throat.

'Charles Daly,' he said. 'Charlie, actually. And I'm seventy- …'

He paused and smiled.

'Just say I'm old!'

The girl smiled.

'So, Mr Daly, what was it like growing up in Dublin back then?'

'Ah, call me Charlie. I haven't been called Mr Daly for years! Well, it was harder in some places. You take Billy Scott. He lived on a nice road near Croke Park, lovely redbrick houses. Fitzroy Avenue. He was so close to Croke Park, he could kick a ball and hit the gate of the place. Little shop across the way. Same as me. We lived on Clare Road, you know?'

The student nodded. 'In the city?'

'It is now, but not then. We lived in fields, near farms. Sure, it was a lovely quiet place most of the time. Back then, the houses were basic enough, nothing fancy. But we had the city and country, you see? We could do a bit of farm work to make a few pennies if we wanted, and then we had all the shops on our doorstep to spend our pennies. It was great.'

'And you went to school with John William Scott?'

'Yes. We were in the same class. We called him Billy. His brother was Frederick. Fred, they called him. He was a year behind us then. So he was very close to the school as well. They lived on Fitzroy Avenue.'

'Number 15?' the student added.

'Number 15,' said Charles. 'Just over from the shop. They were lovely people. His father was a spirit clerk. You know what they are?'

'Not an idea.'

'Ah, you do! He worked in a distillery, where they made whiskey. Jameson's, I think. He was John. He was a Dublin man. And Billy's grandfather worked as a printer.

'And his mother was Mary. She was from Kildare, from near Naas. Her father lived with them in the house. Now, he was a character. John Chapman was his name. He was a sergeant in the Somerset Regiment. I'll always remember that.'

'And did you visit much?'

'Ach, not really. It wasn't a million miles away, but Clare Road to Fitzroy Avenue wasn't a short hop either. We'd meet in school. And we'd knock around the place a bit. Into the city and out the country like. Sure, looking back now, you'd think every day was an adventure.'

'So where was school? What was that like?'

'St Patrick's in Drumcondra. I remember the big yard. It had parallel bars, like you'd see for gymnastics, and you'd swing off them and do exercises. We'd do synchronised exercises in the yard there, you know? You'd have your stick and it'd be all ...'

Charlie stood up quickly from his chair and stuck his arms forward, like he was holding an imaginary stick. He began performing a routine, moving it around his body like a soldier drilling with a gun.

'And we'd do all this stuff,' he said.

'Well, you didn't forget it anyway, Charlie!' said the girl.

'Ah sure, we did it so much it was stuck into us. And God help you if you didn't get it right! We had a school uniform. It was a dark colour, breeches just below the knee and black stockings. The jacket was dark as well and a white shirt underneath. And that was it really.'

Charlie bowed his head, then looked out the window. He could see the breeze gently lifting the leaves on the tree outside.

'They were hard times too. There was a lot of trouble going on and sometimes it came to your door. I remember the story of poor Professor Carolan. He lived a small bit away from us. He taught in the teacher training college, but this particular time he was looking after Dan Breen and Sean Treacy. Did you ever hear of them?'

'The IRA men?'

'That's them. They were famous even back then. Well, they'd been causing havoc around Dublin with Collins's Squad, killing policemen and all. They were the ones who had started off the War of Independence in Tipperary, when they killed those RIC fellas who were minding a cart of gelignite.'

'At Soloheadbeg?'

'That's right. Sure, everything started then after that. Now they were in Dublin on the run, and they were there when the police raided Professor Carolan's. He was shot and killed, but the lads escaped. Breen, I remember, jumped through a window and down into a conservatory below. Cut his feet on the glass, so he did. He was destroyed.

'Treacy, being the clever one, jumped down through the hole in the glass made by Breen. And they managed to get away. I think they even pipped a couple of the agents who were after them as well.'

The student's eyes were wide with amazement.

'But they got Treacy in the end. He was killed on Talbot Street, in the middle of the city, soon enough after that. Breen got away alright, wrote his book and all. But I don't know if you ever escape those memories. I don't know. Some people are built for that type of stuff. But not everyone is.'

'Did you ever see him?'

'Who?'

'Breen. Or Treacy.'

'Ah sure, if I did I wouldn't have known them! There were no photographs or anything back then. That was half the problem for the British, you see. It was all grand trying to track down Michael Collins and all these IRA men, but sure no one knew what they looked like!'

The room went silent for a few seconds. The student cleared her throat.

'Charlie, would you mind going back to the day now? Back to Bloody Sunday?'

Charlie looked out the window again. Talking about Breen and Treacy felt like he was reading a story from a book. It almost didn't feel like it happened five minutes from his house. Now the face of his friend was on his mind again. A picture of Croke Park flashed through his memory. He remembered the shouting and the noise. His tummy started fluttering with nerves again. He felt afraid. A lifetime had passed since that day, but he still felt afraid.

CHAPTER NINE

PERRY

'Move along, young Robinson! Wake up will ya!'

I was standing in line in the yard behind the tenement with a bucket, waiting to get water from the tap. I was half-asleep – sure, Lord knows what time I had eventually dozed off last night, but I was still listening to all these conversations going on above my head.

The sun was shining, but it was still fairly chilly standing in the shadow of the tall building. I was thinking about football and Croke Park, about maybe charming an apple or an orange from one of the women selling fruit outside. Then getting a good spot up in the tree, above the whole crowd if I was lucky.

But the talk above me was getting into my head. People were talking about gun shots from the Gresham Hotel that morning. It was only down the street from us, on Sackville Street.

'It was the IRA,' the woman in front of me said to the woman standing behind me in the queue.

'Shot them all in their beds. Wait till you see, the Tans and the Auxies will be swarming round before dinner time.

'If they take Sean again, I don't know what I'll do. He was black and blue when he came home the last time.'

We shuffled forward a little. The other woman nodded. 'So who was killed?'

'In the hotel? I don't know. British spies, they're saying. Michael Collins and his men killed all the spies.'

The woman frowned and lowered her voice. 'God love us. And you know what's coming? We're the ones who have to live with the damage.'

'I suppose,' replied the other woman.

'Suppose?! It's grand, all this dying for Ireland, but what about the rest of us? Living in filth for Ireland? Getting battered for Ireland? What about us?'

'For God's sake, Mary,' the other woman replied. 'Mind what you say. They'll shave your head for less.'

She was next to the tap. I was looking up at her when some water sloshed out of her bucket onto my shoes. The woman glared down, catching me looking at her.

'What are you looking at? Mind your business, Perry!'

Someone else in the queue shouted from behind me.

'Young Robinson! Hurry up or move along!'

I filled my bucket with water and went upstairs. When I opened the door, my mother and father were talking about the shooting as well. They didn't see me at first.

'Where was Sam this morning?' my ma asked my da.

'I don't know,' said Da. 'Don't want to know.'

Sam. Cousin Sam. Let me tell you about my cousin Sam.

Jeremiah, that was his real name. 'I love Zambuck soap,' he told me once. 'It's great to soften the legs and keep them light for football.'

So he became 'Zam', which then became 'Sam'.

Sam was fifteen, a few years older than me. His brother Christy was seventeen. Their father was dead and their mother sold fish in the markets near home. The boys played soccer, but they were pure rebels, the pair of them.

It was like there was no escape from that kind of thinking for some people. They were going to be pulled into the fight whether they liked it or not. During the rebellion in 1916, a group of British soldiers near their house started firing on a crowd of locals and killed some unarmed men and boys. I don't remember any of that – I was only six or so – but Sam and Christy would have known all about it. They might even have seen it happen.

The boys might have known some of the ones that died. Might have been their friends. All the people who lived near them knew those ones. Seeing that stuff and living with that memory, it sits in you. It grows something inside you.

So a few years later, in 1919, Sam goes looking to fight for the IRA.

'Sure, he went looking for Michael Collins himself,' my da said once.

'Collins told him to get off home. He wasn't running a nursery.'

But Sam wouldn't go home. Soon enough, he was keeping lookout for the men in Collins's Squad whenever they were around the area. The Squad were a special group of fellas who slipped around the city taking out people the IRA wanted gone. You'd see them round here a bit sometimes. They wore long coats to hide their guns underneath. Peter the Painters, they called the guns.

Christy was in the IRA too. A couple of months ago, Christy and a few lads attacked a police lorry stopped at a bakery on Church Street, just over the road from home. But there were more soldiers than they expected.

And when the fight started, the IRA guns jammed and all the IRA lads scattered. Everyone got away except one lad, who got dragged out by the soldiers from where he was hiding underneath the truck. Kevin Barry, his name was. He was hanged afterwards – barely eighteen and still in school.

So that's why my ma and da were worried about Sam. If the IRA were out attacking all these people this morning, was Sam with them?

Da turned to me and looked at me hard.

'If you're goin' to that match later, be careful, right? You know the drill?'

'Yeah,' I replied.

'Straight to the game.'

'Yeah.'

'Home for the rosary.'

'For the rosary, yeah.'

'No messing with the boys. Who are ya goin' with?'

'Dunno, probably just myself.'

'To the crook in the tree?'

'The tree, yeah.'

I started smiling. My father's face darkened again. I knew he was only worried I might get caught up in some trouble, but I wasn't afraid. I had seen plenty of skirmishes with the Tans around home. There was an old prison near the church opposite us on Halston Street that had been turned into a police station. Being around the Tans was like handling an angry dog, I heard a fella say once. The barking was all noise. You just needed to spot the moment it turned from a bark to a growl.

That was the time to run.

'Don't mess! There's gonna be more Tans and more soldiers out. Things are gonna get messy. Just get up there, get back and stay outta trouble. Right?'

'Will do,' I replied.

Part of me was almost excited about it all. I knew in my bones that Sam was somewhere in the middle of it all, plotting and planning and stealing away on an ambush. Police didn't bother with kids anyway. My father's voice jolted me out of my thoughts.

'So when are you off?' he said. 'What time is the match?'

'It's at quarter to three.'

'Just be careful, will ya?'

His face softened a little around the eyes.

'Just be careful, Perry.'

After Mass across the square on Halston Street, we went back home and my mother got us some food to eat. There was milk and bread, and a little fish left over from the previous day. When it was time to go, I danced down the dark stairs of the building and out into the bright sunlight.

It nearly blinded me.

When I stopped squinting, I saw a horse and cart trotting towards me. I jumped back out of the way as it swept past. Then I saw Jack. Apples Jack, from yesterday.

'Sweet suffering damnation, Robinson!' he shouted across the road. 'Are ya blind or wha'?'

I smiled back, especially when his mother gave him a slap across the back of the head for using curse words. I started running up the street.

'And listen to me, young Robinson!' shouted Jack's ma when she saw me. 'Mind you don't end up like your uncle! There's police everywhere! Where's your cousin?'

I kept running, but I frowned at her as I sprinted past. That was a mean thing for her say about Uncle William.

Imagine being the type of person to say a thing like that. People can be terrible cruel.

CHAPTER TEN

JEROME

Jerry's dad hurried away from Blessington Street towards Sackville Street. He was there within a few minutes, rushing past the Gresham Hotel, sitting grandly in the centre of the city. He noticed a cluster of soldiers and police milling around, guarding the entrance after the shootings that morning, but his eyes were trained on the tram lines. He was watching for the next carriage heading south across the River Liffey.

It was past midday when he jumped on board. The trams were busy, bringing people in all directions around Dublin. The weather was still bright, offering a rare opportunity in November for city people to escape to the beaches before the winter chill set in again.

He heard snatches of the same conversation around him. People talked in murmurs and whispers.

'My Alfie heard from the policeman next door, they went to houses on Mount Street,' said one woman. 'Pembroke Street, Ranelagh Road. All close together. Sure, you saw the crowd outside the Gresham? Another bunch there. Shot in their beds! Imagine.'

A voice was speaking quietly behind him.

'There'll be trouble. When the police are hit, it's the people that suffer next.'

The tram crossed the Liffey, trundling up the road to the broad bend in front of Trinity College. Jerome jumped off on Dame Street and walked quickly up the street towards the Castle.

The Castle. That was all anyone called it. For nearly 800 years, Dublin Castle had been the seat of British rule in Ireland. It was the Empire's Irish anchor, driven deep into the country.

From here, the great tentacles of government reached out and wrapped around every part of the land. Civil servants worked in the offices. Soldiers and police used the Castle as barracks. The Chief Secretary for Ireland, the Lord Chancellor and the Attorney General for Ireland – the British government's most important levers of power in Ireland – were all based here. The head of the military in Ireland, General Sir Nevil Macready, operated from the Castle.

It was a place of high walls and secrets. In 1916, a group of rebels had almost taken the Castle on the first day of the Rising, but unsure about how many soldiers were stationed inside, they held back.

'Cowards!' Jerome remembered a soldier remarking loudly in the Castle canteen once, retelling the story of that day to a group of new arrivals. 'Not a soldier among them with the courage to seize the moment.'

But the country felt different now. After all the rebel leaders had been executed, they had become heroes to the people. Many rebels had come home from prisons in England the following year and joined Sinn Féin or went back fighting with the IRA. They staged ambushes and attacked police and army patrols, before disappearing again like ghosts.

The mood in the country was changing. Jerome felt it. The people who worked in the Castle had never been overly friendly, but he could have sworn some of them were now finding ways to treat him even more coldly. People spoke more cautiously around him. Whatever it was, everything in his calm, ordered life felt more and more uncertain.

Jerome walked on up the hill from the tram. In front of the Castle, fanned out across the top of the street, stood a wall of people, all of them pushing and shoving towards the front gates. He swerved and squeezed through the crowd. The ones at the back were shouting.

'Come on, push up! Let us in!'

'For God's sake let us in!'

'Save us!'

'Don't leave us here! You can't leave us here!'

The people in the middle of the crowd were stuck, unable to go forwards or backwards.

Jerome nudged and shifted his body sideways, ducked under arms and reached his arms over others as he waded through the throng, towards the line of soldiers in front of the Castle gates. He finally got near the front. The huge, solid steel gates were closed. Soldiers sat in their perches high above, guns trained on the crowd.

He jostled his arms to make an inch of space and managed to reach inside his jacket pocket to pull out an identity card. Jerome shouted at the soldier nearest to him.

'Excuse me! Hey! Look here!'

The soldier glanced at him and looked away again.

'No! Look here! I need to get inside!'

'They all think they need to get inside, mate.'

Jerome waved the card.

'But see here! I've been summoned!'

The soldier scowled and walked over, pulling the card from Jerome's hand. He looked at him again.

'Alright! Come through! Get that man through the line!'

Another soldier, bigger and burlier than the first one, threw his rifle strap onto his shoulder and grabbed Dad by both jacket lapels. He lifted Jerome out of the crowd like he was pulling him from a swamp.

'Thank you,' said Jerome.

'Now clear off!' the soldier replied, handing him back his card.

CHAPTER ELEVEN

Jerome O'Leary stood for a moment in the open space between the line of soldiers and the gate to the Castle courtyard and looked back at the panicking crowd. Men, women and children; families clinging together, seeking refuge. The faces of the people at the front were stricken with terror.

A similar scene took his breath away as he walked across the courtyard. It was quieter, but the air still seemed full of fear.

Families who had made it inside huddled together, talking in urgent, hushed tones among themselves. RIC police officers, and the Auxiliaries and Black and Tans brought from Britain to help them, were moving around between the various groups. If families looked frightened, it seemed to make the police furious.

Jerome saw Lacey, another man from his office, across the courtyard. He nodded in his direction. Lacey paced towards him.

'Good. You got in. It's chaos out there.'

'What in the name of God is going on outside? Who are all those people?'

'They're civil servants, secretaries, anyone working for the Crown,' Lacey said. 'When word started going round that the IRA had done in a load of spies, anyone working here started turning up with their families, looking to get in. They're all terrified that the IRA will be coming after them.'

'Good God!' Jerome said. 'Spies? Are they going after everyone?'

'No one knows,' Lacey said, pulling Jerome by the arm and leading him out of the courtyard towards the door that led to the offices. 'I'm only hearing whispers on the corridor; I don't think the British themselves know how many have been killed. I was in early this morning to finish some work and I saw the head of the Auxiliaries, you know … Crozier?'

Jerome nodded.

'He arrived in his car. Apparently he saw two Auxies killed over near Mount Street. IRA put them up against a wall and shot them. They had already killed another man in his bed. The word coming down from the intelligence offices then was sixty killed.'

'Sixty!' Jerome's mind was racing, full of questions.

'They're figuring out a plan now,' Lacey said. 'Whatever comes next, they're going somewhere.'

'They?' said Jerome.

'The Black and Tans. The Auxiliaries. Whatever about spies being killed, two of their own got pipped. They won't rest after this. That's why they sent for you.'

Jerome frowned.

'Me? What have I to do with any of this?'

'They're interrogating everyone,' Lacey replied. 'Any Irish working here. I've gotten grilled already.'

'What sort of things are they asking?' Jerome asked, his face darkening.

'They're looking for any type of information on the IRA. Did we see anything? Did we hear anything? Did we leak information on where these men lived? That sort of thing.'

'But I ... how could I ...?'

Jerome paused. He could feel every muscle in his body tighten with anxiety. He took a deep breath to ward away the fear.

'What do I know? Nothing! What can I tell them? Nothing!'

Lacey's eyes softened. He placed a steadying hand on Jerome's shoulder.

'Just calm down. I know you're not involved. I'm not either. This is them in a panic. Who knows how many men were taken out? Six? Sixty? It doesn't really matter. Look around at this mayhem. It worked. What we need now in order to survive is calm. Answer their questions carefully. Be short. The truth is, you have no knowledge about this at all, right?'

Lacey pointed at a window on the second floor of a nearby building.

'I heard an Auxie up there in his rooms shot himself this morning, because he might have given up the address of one of these boys to some IRA man by accident. People's heads are spinning.'

73

Jerome looked round again. Police and soldiers were scurrying everywhere. He could hear the rumble of the Crossley Tender trucks as their engines started up.

'Come on,' said Lacey. 'Let's go to the office.'

Jerome hadn't even noticed they had left the maze of corridors within the Castle and reached their office. It was quiet and cool. Sunlight streamed in through the small window, spreading a soft, low light. Lacey opened the bottom drawer of his desk and pulled out a bottle of whiskey and two small glasses.

'I think we need something medicinal,' he said. He began pouring.

'So, they've put as many people from outside on the street as they can into the barracks here, but it's full up now. The next plan is to try to house all those people outside in some hotels around the place. It's a mess. Total mess.'

Jerome took the glass. 'It's worrying is what it is. Very worrying. What's coming next?'

Lacey swished the whiskey gently around his glass. 'The country is changing, Jerome. The English don't want to be here anymore and more of our own people are driving hard now to get them out. After 800 years, the grip is loosening. But that bit before you finally let go, maybe that's when you grip the hardest.'

Lacey raised his glass. 'We'll drink to survival, whatever happens. To possessing cool enough heads to survive.'

Dad sat still, gazing out the window at the bewildering mix of terrified civilians and angry, bellowing soldiers and police storming around the courtyard. He thought of home.

He thought of Jerry and the match he hoped would never be.

'To survival,' he said, and swallowed his drink in one gulp.

CHAPTER TWELVE

Mary Angela O'Leary had come back from the nearest street corner with a newspaper. She ran upstairs and bolted through the door to her mother.

'Something happened, ma,' she said. 'The newspaper boys are saying Michael Collins and the IRA have done in a load of spies all over the city.'

Her mother sat at the table as Mary told her the news, then bowed her head. Jerry was sitting on his dad's chair, pondering.

'Do you think he'll have to stay in the Castle?' he wondered out loud to no one in particular. Jerry's mother and Mary knew he was talking about father, but no one answered.

Eventually, his mother stood up.

'Come on,' she said. 'The dinner won't cook itself and he'll be starving whenever he gets home. Mary, give me a hand. Jerry, stay in the house and don't make a mess of your clothes.'

Jerry frowned. It was after one o'clock. He was hungry, but he was also thinking about Croke Park.

His mother washed potatoes and placed them in a pot of water simmering on the stove. A lump of bacon was already boiling. Steam filled up the room as the water bubbled and popped in the pot. Mary went to open a window.

'Don't!' her mother cried. 'We'll all have the flu by Tuesday!'

Jerry had escaped to the bedroom, but was now being tortured by the smell of potatoes almost boiled and the salty scent of bacon.

'Oh, I can't take this anymore,' he said quietly and bounded back into the kitchen. 'Is it ready?'

Mary scowled at him again.

'Nearly,' said his mother. I've set the table. I know your match is on. If your father isn't home, I'll make you a plate and you can go.'

'But I'm so starving!'

'Now, don't be cheeky, Jerry!' his mother said. 'Be glad of what you get when you get it!'

Jerry glanced at the clock again. It was heading for two o'clock now. The newspaper the previous day had said the game was starting at 2.45pm. Plenty of time yet, he thought. Still, if he didn't eat soon, he wasn't sure he'd survive till then.

Finally, at ten minutes past two, everything was ready.

'Do you want to eat now, Mary?' her mother asked.

'I'll wait,' Mary said, and left the kitchen to avoid the sound of her brother's munching.

'There you go, Jerry,' his mother said, placing a clean white dinner plate in front of him with two peeled potatoes, two slices of bacon and a spoon of bright, green cabbage. She poured out a mug of milk for him and placed it on the table.

Then she leaned back against the sink and gazed at him, smiling.

'Happy now?'

Jerry smiled back. He ate so fast, it was all gone in five minutes. 'That was …'

He couldn't find the words.

He looked at his mother and smiled again. 'Thank you,' he said. She smiled back.

'You're welcome.'

He looked at the clock. It was nearly twenty past two. Jerry knew for sure now, there would be no Dad and no chocolate. No stories on the way to Croke Park and no smell of pipe smoke today.

His father often told him about watching Cork's footballers. They played in blue, with a huge gold 'C' on their front. But since the year before, 1919, they had red jerseys. Something about the Army coming to their offices in Cork city and stealing their blue jerseys, his father told him.

But the red ones were doing them no harm. Cork won an All-Ireland hurling title in 1919. 'It's like a taste of home,' his father had said that evening.

But now the Castle had him. The mere word 'Castle' made Jerry seethe with fury.

Jerry had visited with him once. It was a forbidding sort of place, with its high walls and gates, like those severe, brooding fortresses in his adventure books.

The soldiers had growled at his father when he showed his identity card to enter. The Auxiliaries and Black and Tans inside the Castle were a mess of uniforms and accents. Some wore kilts. All of them swore and walked like they were clenched up inside with anger, ready to fight at any moment.

On the day Jerry was there, two of them had walked towards Jerry and his dad as they crossed the courtyard to the office. One was tall and broad, wearing a dark navy uniform with a harp insignia on his cap. Jerry recognised the uniform – he was an Auxiliary.

The other one was shorter and heavier, with a ruddy face and a thick brown moustache. He spat on the ground in front of him. Jerry felt nervous.

As they passed by, the taller one walked slightly into Dad's path, banging his shoulder against him. Jerome lost his balance, bouncing against Jerry who was walking alongside. He dropped the folders of paper in his hand and they scattered all over the cobbles.

'Keep to your side of the courtyard, Irish,' the Auxiliary bellowed as he walked past. The other one cackled with laughter. Jerry was filled with anger.

'I'll help, Dad,' he said, bending down to pick up the papers as they threatened to blow away. Jerry glared at the men as they strode off.

'No need, Jerry,' his father said. 'No need.'

He looked up at the backs of the two soldiers, then he looked Jerry in the eye.

'Just ignore them. You'll meet ignorant people in every walk of life.'

Dad's office was dull, filled with desks and the clackety-clack sound of typewriters and telephone conversations. The walls were pale blue and sad-looking.

They had stayed an hour while Jerome did some paper-work, then went for tea and a cake at a café nearby. Jerry never wished to visit the Castle again. And now the place had swallowed his father up again on a Sunday morning.

He did some sums in his head. How long could he wait? The game was due to begin in twenty-five minutes. It would take that long to get up to Croke Park and into the game.

His mother interrupted his thoughts. 'Are you worried about your dad, Jerry?'

'No,' he replied. 'It's just … the game. I don't want to go without him, and what if he comes home and I'm gone?'

His mother folded her arms and sighed. 'I know, pet,' she said. 'His work is very demanding. On all of us. But he does his best. You know that, don't you?'

'Yes, Ma,' Jerry replied.

His mother sat down across from him at the table. She reached over to lift his chin up with her finger.

'I'm not sure what to tell you, Jerry. If you want to go to the game, I know your father won't mind if you go without him. But there's been a lot of trouble today already. I'm really not sure you should go at all …'

His mother's words made Jerry worry even more. Whatever about not going with his father, now he was in danger of missing the game entirely.

'But, Ma, I'll meet up with a few other lads from school. I'm old enough now to get up and home. There'll be no trouble at all. I'll be grand!'

Jerry's mother sat back in the chair, thinking. A few seconds of silence passed like hours.

'If you go,' she said. 'I want you back here straight away afterwards. If you go up the top of the road and see soldiers, I want you back straight away.'

She stood up, but she didn't stop talking.

'If you see Black and Tans, I want you back straight away.

'If you see trouble on the road down, I want you back straight away.

'If you get into the ground and something happens, I want you back straight away.'

She fixed him with a stare. 'Do you understand? Be as careful as you've ever been, Jerry.'

'I understand, Ma,' Jerry said solemnly.

He got up from the table. His mother walked over and hugged him tightly.

'Just be careful, Jerry, that's all.'

'I know,' he said, 'I will.'

He found his coat hanging on the back of the door, and tucked a cap into his pocket. His mother followed him out to the landing. Jerry looked back at her.

'Tell Da I said a little prayer for a draw,' he said.

He smiled again at her. She smiled back and returned inside. Jerry ran downstairs and put his hands in his pockets before he opened the front door, feeling around for the penny he needed to get into Croke Park. He tried his trouser pockets, then his cardigan pockets. Nothing.

He sensed someone staring at him. It was Mary, standing at the top of the stairs.

'What?'

'You lost something?'

'No,' Jerry replied. 'I just can't *find* something.'

Mary sighed again and disappeared back behind the door. She sighs so much, Jerry sometimes thought, it's a wonder she ever has any time for actual breathing. This time, she was back in a few seconds and bounced down the stairs.

'Here,' she said, stopping one step from the bottom, opening her hand to reveal a penny. 'You'll need that.'

Jerry's face beamed with happiness. He looked at his sister, a little more softly this time.

'Thanks Mary. Ah …' he paused, seeking the right words.

'You're not the worst. And your cabbage was lovely.'

Mary raised her eyes to heaven and sighed again, but it was a different sigh this time. The kind of sigh you give when you see the funny side of something or someone, the side of someone that makes you feel good about being around them.

'Go on,' she said. 'Enjoy the match.'

'I will!' smiled Jerry.

She ran back upstairs. Jerry opened the front door and stepped out into the brilliant sunshine again. He could see the crowds at the top of the street, heading for Croke Park.

Then he slammed the door shut behind him.

CHAPTER THIRTEEN

BILLY

By mid-afternoon, the streets around Croke Park were filled with people. Billy Scott looked out his front door, scanning the passing faces for Charlie.

'Come on, will ya?' he thought. 'It's not that far of a walk from home.'

The shout came from the kitchen.

'Billy! Bring this tea into your grandad.'

Billy threw his eyes to heaven. If it wasn't Charlie Daly humming and hawing his way down from Clare Road, it was Grandad Chapman and his tea.

He could shout back that his brother Fred could bring him the tea, but that might only get him a clip on the ear. Or worse, no match.

'Coming!' he called back.

Billy's mother had the cup of tea poured out on the counter. 'He's in the parlour, Billy,' she said.

'I know,' he replied with a mild scowl.

'Easy,' said his father, looking up at Billy from his newspaper. 'You'll be gone for the afternoon, remember.'

'Sorry, Da,' Billy replied. This was no time to get on the wrong side of anyone.

The cup tottered slightly on the saucer as Billy opened the door to the parlour. His grandfather was sitting on an armchair, gazing out the window.

'Billy!' Grandad smiled. 'Are you still here? Should you not be at your game now?'

'I'm still waiting for Charlie to come, Grandad.'

'And will you win today?'

'Hope so. Tipperary are good, but Dublin should be better. Sure, they're in the All-Ireland final.'

'I see, and Tipperary …?'

'I dunno actually. I'll have to ask Da.'

'Well, I imagine it'll be a fine encouragement to Dublin if they do win,' said his grandad. 'Have you time to sit?'

Billy glanced nervously out the window. Still no sign of Charlie.

'I do, I suppose,' he replied.

He wondered what Grandad was thinking. Was he going to start telling his old stories? When Billy was younger, Grandad's stories of his years as a soldier seemed thrilling. Now he was fourteen, they were starting to sound old and repetitive.

'They shipped us off to South Africa,' he would begin. 'The Zulu War, against the natives. Great warriors they were, brave and noble people. But they were no match for our muskets.'

He would tell him about the sea voyage to South Africa. 'Whales and porpoises,' he'd exclaim, 'and so many flying fish, they could have leapt onto the deck with us!'

Grandad was English. 'I was a sergeant in the Somerset Regiment. Born in Wantage,' he would tell Billy. 'Near Oxford. Where I grew up, there was a convent that once housed the greatest number of nuns in the world. That's the truth! So many nuns shuffling about in their habits. We couldn't walk the streets for nuns!'

Grandad had come to Ireland after the Zulu War and married Billy's grandmother in Kildare. He came to live at Fitzroy Avenue with Billy's ma and da when Billy's grandmother died. Billy was just a baby then.

He had known his grandad all his life. He knew his stories and his ways and his kindnesses. But Grandad looked at Billy now in a way that told Billy he wasn't going to tell him his old stories. His voice was soft, almost sad.

'From the day I landed in Ireland, Billy, I found happiness. I married your grandmother, and your mother's birth brought us such joy. And I have seen disturbances and trouble in the country before. I've had to quieten a few fellows down the years, I can tell you.

'But nowadays, people are angrier. Soldiers and policemen are angrier. I shudder sometimes at the things I hear and the stories I read in the newspapers. These Sinn Féiners are determined to take over. I fear they won't stop at anything.'

Billy looked quizzically at the old man.

'What is it, Grandad?'

'Did you hear what happened this morning?'

'Was there more trouble?'

'Yes, there was. Many important men were killed today. Men of great value. This will not go unpunished, Billy.'

He placed his hand on Billy's arm and squeezed. He looked gravely at his grandson.

'None of us knows what our future holds, Billy, but please be careful today. If you see police or soldiers, come back home. Promise me that, Billy.'

Billy nodded. 'I will, Grandad. I'll be careful. Promise.'

His grandfather paused and smiled as he looked out the window. 'Good lad, good lad. My word, the crowd is gathering out there. You mightn't even get in!'

'I know,' Billy sighed. 'Charlie'd better hurry or I'll be off. See you later, Grandad.'

'Good boy, Billy,' the old man smiled. 'Good boy.'

Billy ran to the hall and opened the front door again. Still no sign of Charlie. He was due ten minutes ago. If Billy waited any longer, he might miss the start.

Luckily, having Croke Park right at the end of his road gave Billy more time than most people to get to the game. When Billy looked out on a regular morning, he could see the row of houses right in front of the sports ground. The local boys slipped in and played football games whenever they could.

Sometimes the dressing rooms might be open from a game that weekend, with a forgotten pair of shorts or a sliotar, a special ball for hurling, left behind. Little bits and pieces of treasure for the local boys – one of the blessings of living so close to the place.

He was walking back to the kitchen when there was a knock on the front door.

Finally.

Billy went back and opened it. Charlie slipped into the hall and took off his cap.

'Jeepers, it's crazy out there! Took me ages to get through the crowd. Lord, Billy, you're dressed up like you're goin' dancing!'

'Wha'?'

Charlie grabbed his tie and ruffled it out from beneath his jumper.

'Very handsome,' he said. 'Who are you trying to impress?'

'No one,' scowled Billy. 'And anyway, you're late. What were ya doin'? Milkin' cows or something?'

'Clown.' Charlie smiled. 'So are we goin'?'

'Come in for a second. I just have to get me coat and a few bits.'

'Alright,' said Charlie. 'Howya, Mrs Scott. Fred.'

Billy's brother was sitting at the table, rolling a small ball from one hand to the other.

'Goin' to the match, Charlie?' Fred asked.

'Yeah.'

'You're late. What were ya doin' up there? Chasing chickens or somethin'?'

'Fred,' scolded his mother.

'But Clare Road, Ma! They're all farmers up there. Muck up to their ears!'

'That's enough, Fred,' said his dad. 'Go on, go upstairs and leave the lad be.'

Fred made a face at Charlie. Charlie stuck his leg out as Fred left the room, but pulled it back just before he tripped him. He heard Billy galloping down the stairs.

'Right, we're off,' he called from the hall.

His father followed Charlie out and put his hand on Billy's shoulder.

'Before ye go, lads, listen: just be careful. There was a lot of trouble in town this morning. There'll be police around. Just go over the road to the match and then come back. Charlie, you can have your tea here, and then we'll see about getting you home.'

'Yes, Dad,' replied Billy.

'Have you money?'

'Yes, Dad.'

'And your glasses?'

'Yes, Dad.'

'I like your tiepin, Billy,' chuckled Charlie. Billy had taken steps to make sure he couldn't mess up his tie again.

'Shut up, Charlie.'

'That's enough, Billy,' frowned his dad. 'Just be careful, boys, that's all.'

'We will, Dad,' said Billy. 'Promise.'

'Goodbye, Mrs Scott,' Charlie called.

She waved from the kitchen. 'Have a good time, boys.'

'Come on,' whispered Charlie under his breath. 'You're making us late.'

Billy glared back. '*I'm* making us late?! Just move!'

CHAPTER FOURTEEN

Billy shut the front door behind him and the boys were immediately swallowed up by a swarm of people.

'Mother of Moses!' said Charlie. His cap was knocked from his head by a passer-by rushing along through the crowd. He picked it up before anyone could knock him over.

'This is mad. What's the plan, Billy?'

'Usual,' Billy replied. 'We'll go in by Mr O'Toole's house at the corner and see can we get up on the canal wall.'

'Sounds fair,' Charlie replied. 'Want an apple?'

'Orange,' said Billy.

Charlie looked around for one of the women who sold fruit from big wicker baskets. He spotted one through the forest of people and dodged across to her.

'Can I have one apple and one orange please?'

'Here ya go, son,' she replied. Charlie handed her a couple of coins.

'Up for the day from Tipperary, are ya?'

'Wha? No, I'm from over there!' Charlie said, pointing towards Fitzroy Avenue.

'Oh,' frowned the woman. 'Coulda sworn ya had a country accent. You're not a farmer, are ya?'

'No!' said Charlie. This was worse than Fred in the kitchen. He didn't want to lose his temper, but he was close.

'Thanks for the fruit.'

Billy couldn't contain his laughter. 'Pure farmer, you,' he roared. 'Pure farmer! All the way up from Tipperary!'

Billy howled with laughter and lifted Charlie's hand up in the air.

'Hey! Will someone bring this lad back to Thurles?!!!'

'Shut up, Billy,' glared Charlie, pulling his hand down. 'Don't push it! Just don't!'

Tears were streaming down Billy's face. He took off his glasses and wiped his eyes.

'Aw, that was the best! Just the best!'

'Come on,' said Charlie, nodding towards the thick queue trailing back from the turnstiles, trying to change the subject quickly as he could. He could only imagine the stories Billy would tell at school tomorrow.

'Get your money ready. We'll get in here.'

JERRY

The crowds at the top of Blessington Street were pouring into the roads towards Croke Park. The sun was still shining brightly and the pace was brisk.

From the top of the hill by Mountjoy Square, Jerry could see right down to Croke Park below. The road was flooded with people. It was getting late and the crowds were stream-ing into the alleys leading to the turnstiles, the queues snaking back onto Jones' Road.

Jerry slipped through the crowd, veering like an eel around the mess of legs and arms. He made it through the turnstiles by the canal bridge, but was met by a solid wall of people inside the ground.

He was pushed and squeezed and carried almost off his feet onto the bank behind the goal, the blare of the brass band playing on the field muffled by the bodies surrounding him. For a minute, the fresh air and sunlight of a crisp November day had disappeared.

All he could smell now was sweat and beer and cigarette smoke and stale coats.

He finally found a pocket of space in a forest of strangers. He couldn't see over their shoulders or through the little gaps between them. He was afraid to ask anyone to move.

Who knew what they might do if he did?

Suddenly he felt two hands catching him beneath his arm-pits and lifting him out of the crowd, landing him roughly onto the wall. A man looked up at him, smiling.

'There ya go, young fella,' he said. 'Best seat in the house.'

'Thank you,' replied Jerry, still shy but grateful. He looked across the field, bathed now in sunshine and dotted with play-ers. He could see the Tipperary team, in their white jerseys with a green hoop, the word 'Tipperary' stitched in gold thread on the front. Some of them were kicking a football between them. He saw one player talking to a priest over by the grandstand.

Then he looked further outfield to the Dublin players. He saw Paddy McDonnell, tall and regal, like a king of all he surveyed. He was standing in the middle of the field, nodding and smiling at the referee.

Frank Burke was further up the field, closer to the goal kicking the ball to one of the Synnott brothers. Their sky-blue jerseys gleamed in the bright sun.

Soon, the players began to gather in the middle of the field. The two teams lined up in their positions facing each other, waiting for the referee to throw the ball in to start the game.

The loud murmur of the crowd gathered up into a full-throated cheer like a rolling wave. Jerry smiled and felt his skin prickle with excitement. It wouldn't be long now.

PERRY

I raced out of Little Britain Street, dodging the puddles and the people, trying not to slip on the cobblestones. Sackville Street was busy with people, queuing for trams or just out on a walk, taking in the fine weather.

Soldiers and Black and Tans still crowded around the Gresham Hotel, where those men were killed this morning.

I ran up the street, catching the odd funny accent as I went. The Tipperary boys were in town alright.

The closer I got to Croke Park, the thicker the crowds became. I was getting worried. Would my spot in the tree still be there for me? I tried to quicken my pace, but there was no way to run, with the wall of people rolling down to the ground.

When I reached the bridge outside Croke Park, I could see the tree up ahead.

Empty. Whew.

That didn't stop me worrying though. What if someone still got there before me? I was so close now.

I tried to push through the crowd even harder, wriggling and slaloming left and right, moving into any space I saw. 'Mind your elbows!' one man shouted at me.

Eventually I was over the bridge. I passed the ticket seller at his table and slipped across to the base of the tree. As I started to climb up into the branches, a few people cheered below me.

'Ha ha! He's got the right idea!'

'Good lad yourself!'

'How much are they charging for those seats?!'

'Mind you don't get hit by an apple, or a ball!'

I kept climbing. In the summertime, when the tree was thick with bright green leaves, you could see nothing from here.

This was the perfect winter's day for the tree, though, just like my da had said. Bright and clear, with the branches dry and clean.

I found my crook and got comfortable, looking down over all the people stuck in queues coming into the ground. I could see all the way across to Hill 60 at the far end. The big mound was packed with people. So was the bank on the other side of the ground.

I looked down and spotted a fruit seller with her basket.

'Rats,' I thought. I had forgotten to get an orange.

I thought about sliding back down the tree, but then I saw the players assembling in the middle of the field. The game was about to start.

Another boy was on the wall near the canal, and I caught his eye for a second. I'd say we were both thinking exactly the same thing. Two small fellas in the middle of all these big people, with the best views in Croke Park, masters of our own day and witnesses to a great adventure about to begin.

I didn't know him, but I know he was feeling just what I was feeling.

CHAPTER FIFTEEN

Jerome stood in the corridor in front of a thick, brown oak door. He took a deep breath, then knocked three times.

'Come in,' said a voice.

Jerome pushed open the door. An officer in khaki-coloured uniform was sitting at a modestly sized desk covered with papers. An ashtray was filled with stubbed-out cigarettes. The air was stale and thick with smoke. The small room had no windows, but a single light bulb hanging from the ceiling and a desk lamp illuminated a mess of ledgers and files. The officer was writing on a piece of paper.

'Sit down, good chap,' he said without looking up. His accent was clipped and formal. 'I'm Evans. I don't think we've met. You're … O'Leary?'

'That's right,' Jerome replied and coughed, the smoke scratching the back of his throat.

'You've got a cold, O'Leary? Late nights and early mornings, eh?'

Why did he ask that? Jerome wondered. Why ask him in that way? Was it a trap, to trick him into saying he was out and about at odd times of the day? Doing what? Meeting whom? The nerves in Jerome's stomach tingled again.

'No, sir, just a winter itch. Nothing more.'

The officer finally looked up from his papers. He gazed evenly at Jerome for a moment. Jerome stared back. Though his face was craggy with worry lines, Jerome didn't imagine the officer was much older than forty-five, maybe fifty. He had a thick moustache and narrow eyes, and his black hair was greying at the temples. His face was puce-red – the product, thought Jerome, of too many brandies and cigarettes.

'I'll get to the point, O'Leary,' he said. 'You'll have heard about the business in the city this morning.'

Jerome didn't reply. The officer looked at him again, more intently this time.

'You have heard, haven't you?'

'Just now, sir. Just when I arrived here.'

'I see. Well, it's a shocking business, which will not go unpunished. Our job is to find the perpetrators and bring them to justice. That is our only intention. Not revenge. Not atrocity. Only justice.

Jerome swallowed nervously. 'I see, sir.'

'So it is to you and others we look for assistance now. The priests say it; many of the Irish leaders say it: This violence has no place here. It has no moral standing. And the men who pulled those triggers this morning, they are not the only ones with blood on their hands now, O'Leary. No. They are but the sharp end of the sword. We seek those who directed them to thrust that sword.'

Jerome began to speak. 'Sir, I don't know what impression you have of me, or what idea you might …'

The officer interrupted. 'To that end, O'Leary, we seek information. Any scrap or shred of information, no matter how modest or small or inconsequential it may seem to you. We seek it. Perhaps you have seen something. Heard something. I see by your address that you live close to the centre of the city. Perhaps you heard something in an alehouse. Or on a tram. Or here?'

Jerome stiffened in his seat. The officer tilted his head to one side and smirked.

'Of course, O'Leary, I don't expect that you had any hand, act or part in these repulsive acts. But perhaps you know something that we do not yet know. Are there men here in this very Castle perverting the future of Ireland itself?'

Jerome cleared his throat nervously. 'Sir, I wouldn't know. I work here as an accountant. I come to work; I go home. I have a wife and two children, sir, I …'

'You see, O'Leary,' the officer interrupted. 'That's the problem with this blasted thing, this revolt … war … murder … whatever you wish to call it. Indeed, what would you call it, O'Leary?'

'Call what, sir?'

The officer's eyes narrowed and spread his arms apart. 'This, O'Leary! All of this! Us! You! Them! This killing; these battles in the countryside.'

He picked up a sheaf of papers and shoved them towards Jerome. 'Every day I receive these reports: burnings, killings, robberies, kidnappings. Every blasted day.'

His tone was changing; he was getting angry. 'What would you call THIS?'

Jerome was suddenly gripped with the terrible feeling that his next words could decide his life.

'Sir. I do not concern myself with matters that do not invade upon my house, my wife and my children. We have lived in Dublin some years now. I have worked loyally at the Castle. All I have ever sought was to provide for my family. The flag under which I live, that is not a priority to me.'

The officer sat back in his chair and sighed. 'So you stand for nothing, O'Leary?'

'I stand for my family, sir. I live for them.'

The officer leaned back in his chair. He rolled his eyes and sighed again, then returned his gaze to the papers in front of him.

'Your friend, Lacey. You know him well?'

'I know him as a work colleague, sir. We share an office. Sometimes we lunch togeth–'

'The people he consorts with,' the officer barked. 'What type?'

'Type … sir?'

The officer glared at Jerome again.

'Yes, man! What type! Who are they? What are their views? Have you seen him in rebel company? Has he views? Or do I need to explain "views" to you as well, man?!'

Jerome suddenly felt confused. Was Lacey the real reason he was here?

'Sir, I only know Mr Lacey as a colleague. I have never socialised with him beyond the Castle. I scarcely know where the man lives.'

'Has he ever spoken to you about new republics or independence?'

'No, sir.'

'Has he any access to personal files? Have you?'

'I do not, sir. Of Mr Lacey, I would imagine not.'

'You imagine not?' said the officer. 'We shall see in due course.'

There was a pause that felt like hours.

'You will provide me with a detailed report of your movements over the past forty-eight hours, O'Leary. Every blasted step since you left here last Friday. I expect it to be delivered to this office by close of business tomorrow, Monday. Is that clear?'

'Yes, sir.'

The officer clasped his hands in front of him, fixing O'Leary with a stare.

'Do you know how many of your type I have had to deal with today? You are a nation with no sense of yourselves.

Yours are people who prefer to shoot from behind hedgerows, wearing the clothes of civilians, then disappear into your hovels and villages when the killing is done, rather than stand and fight.'

Jerome stayed silent, fixing his gaze on the front of the desk, where the light from the lamp yielded to the dark shadow of the wood.

'You and your kind, this god-awful country, will always need a shoulder of a stronger, greater power to lean on. You will never find your way to freedom, because you cannot see beyond your own pitiful needs. Your country may well become yours soon, and perhaps we will be glad to be rid of it, but once you gain that which you yearn for now, your national cowardice will make it impossible for you to ever fully be free.'

The officer closed his eyes.

'Just get out.'

Jerome rushed out and shut the door behind him. The sunlight in the hallway made his eyes hurt. He saw the outline of Lacey walking towards him. Jerome wondered whether he should mention to Lacey that the officer was asking about him. Then he thought again: one wrong word could tangle him up in a story he had no part in.

'How did it go?' Lacey asked.

'I need to get home,' Jerome said. 'I need to go right now.'

He began to walk briskly down the hall towards an exit onto the courtyard. Lacey doubled up his stride to keep pace.

'But what did he ask you? What did you say?'

Jerome continued walking, sternly looking straight ahead.

'Nothing. Nothing unusual anyway. Exactly what you'd imagine: do I know anything, anybody. That sort of thing.'

'And?'

Jerome glanced quickly at Lacey. They were out in the courtyard again, moving through the chaotic clusters of people, heading towards the gate.

'And nothing. I know nothing. I could tell him nothing. But I need to get home now.'

Lacey walked him to the gate, still clogged by the panicking crowd. 'Let this man through!' he said. A soldier turned around.

'I'm sorry sir,' he said. 'Our orders are not to allow anyone out of the Castle once they're in. Security reasons.'

'What are you talking about?' Jerome shouted. 'I must get home!'

The captain in charge of the soldier at the gate heard him shout and strode across. He nodded to the soldier. 'Get back to your post, lad. Now, gentlemen, I am afraid our orders are very clear. Anyone admitted to the safety of the Castle must remain here until this emergency has been brought under control. We cannot have people swanning in and out of here, bringing information to God knows where.'

Jerome's eyes narrowed. He was now glaring at the soldier like the officer had glared at him. 'I am not a spy,' he said. 'For anyone!'

'I don't care what you are, sir,' the captain replied. 'Our orders are clear. Every man, woman and child within these four walls must stay within these four walls. I would suggest you gentlemen make yourselves comfortable. You may be here for some time.'

'But my family …!' began Jerome. But the captain was already walking away.

Jerome and Lacey headed back across the courtyard. Jerome's head was spinning with worry. What about Mary and the children? Would they have the good sense to stay at home? And that match. The match he was meant to see with Jerry. Jerome's face grimaced.

Oh, Jerry.

CHAPTER SIXTEEN

PERRY

The noise just before the game started, God help us it could deafen you. People were crying out for games, see. All the fighting had stopped nearly everything everywhere.

And then this was a game involving these two, Dublin and Tipperary. They were good teams. Really good teams. Dublin were already in the All-Ireland semi-final, but they hadn't won an All-Ireland in … well the last time they did I wasn't born anyway.

And Tipperary? Well, they had reached the final a couple of years ago. I could hear two lads below me putting it all together for themselves.

'This game could tell us a lot,' said one. He had a country sort of accent, so I'm guessing a Tipperary man.

'Ah, it could indeed,' said the other. I recognised that accent: He was a city man, maybe not Little Britain Street though. Somewhere nice. I'd say his house had a garden.

'Look, if Dublin don't win, and it's a while since they beat Tipperary, they'll doubt themselves if they meet them in an All-Ireland final. That's for sure.'

'That was the talk below all week,' said the Tipperary man.

'They came close the couple of years ago, but they need this now. Just to tell themselves they can do it.

'I only decided to come last night, when one of the boys was bringing the car. We fancied a good, long spin. You'd be tired stuck at home, especially with all the trouble.'

'Were the roads bad?'

'Shocking. Sure, where the Army and the Tans weren't patrolling and stopping you, the IRA had blown up bits of the road to stop you moving. It was a curse. And of course there's not a match to watch below there.'

'That's the worst of it,' said the city man. 'And look at the crowd here. People are delighted with it.'

'They are,' said the Tipperary man. 'So long as we win!'

The brass band marched off and the two teams gathered in the centre of the field, lined up alongside each other. This was it. I looked around the field. Every last part of the place was full or filling up quickly. I didn't know the time exactly, but I knew the game was late getting started.

The crowd got louder.

'Come on Dublin!' I shouted at the top of my lungs.

It was a great, free feeling, to shout out loud like that.

All my da's talk about trouble in town, and the soldiers and Tans out on Sackville Street; all the memories in my head about Uncle William and that woman shouting at me about him, and my ma worrying about Sam; all the bangs

and bumps I took to get to my tree; even the orange I forgot
to get – everything in the whole wide world just melted away.

All there was now was the match.

The referee picked the ball up off the ground and threw it
into the air. The players jostled and jumped, trying to catch it.

The crowd roared.

I roared.

The game was on.

* * *

It's funny, when I think of everything that happened once the
game started, I remember certain things so clearly. Like the
tickets being sold outside the ground – they were bright pink.
Bright pink!

I remember the boy sitting on the wall further along. And
the game. You'd think I'd have forgotten all about the game,
but I can see some things like they just happened a second ago.

Maybe it's because of what happened next, but all of these
moments, well, it feels like they happened in slow motion.
It's as if, now that we know what happened, our heads are
trying to hang onto the good memories and not give in to
the bad ones.

The wind was blowing straight down the field from behind
me towards the far end of Croke Park. Dublin were defending

that goal too. I was delighted. That meant Frank Burke was just across from me to the right, where I had a perfect view of him.

The Tipperary fella who was marking him, I heard a man below the tree mention his name.

'The Hogan lad's doing solid work there,' he said.

I didn't really hear much more, but I didn't think anyone would be up to marking the great Frank Burke.

We hardly saw the ball down our end at all. With the wind behind them, Tipperary took over. I couldn't believe it. Paddy McDonnell couldn't catch a ball without getting swamped by Tipperary fellas.

And Johnny, the brother, in goals? Well, he had to make two very good saves. I say they were very good saves, even though I couldn't really see, as they happened way up the other end of the field, but you could tell from the reaction of the crowd and the applause that they must have been good.

It must have been ten minutes or more before the ball came down our way. When we finally did get some action, well, I looked up to the sky and saw something that totally distracted me.

You won't believe what it was.

It was an airplane. An airplane flying over Croke Park! And then it let off a red flare. The crowd cheered. I took off my cap and waved at them. It was so low I could nearly see the pilot inside the plane. Ah, it felt like a rare day then.

The next thing, I heard this sound behind me.

At first, I thought it was trucks rolling over the bridge outside. But even above the noise of the crowd below me, I could hear men shouting.

They sounded angry.

I looked back and saw a line of trucks. A load of men with guns were jumping out and running towards the field.

That's when it happened.

I can't remember if I heard the shot, but it felt like someone punched me so hard on my shoulder that their fist went straight through me into my chest. It blew me out of the tree.

Then I was falling, falling for what seemed like forever. I hit the ground with a horrible thump.

The wind was gone out of me. I was wheezing, trying to catch my breath, and my chest was so heavy it felt like I was pinned to the ground. For a second everything was blurry, then I saw all these legs above me. Over me. Around me. On me.

People were jumping over me and running. Some of them looked down. I looked up at them. I could see it in their eyes, the pure terror.

A few policemen ran past me, firing guns. That's what I remember most, the noise of the guns crackling away and the police shouting at people.

It felt like I was lying there the whole of my life, unable to move, with people leaping over me, trying not to stand on me.

Time seemed to pass so slowly. It felt like the shooting had been stopped for ages, but I could still hear screaming and more and more people were stepping over me. I kept thinking the same thing: Would anyone stop and help me?

Then I felt hands beneath my back and I was scooped up. The man held me and asked my name, but I was lightheaded. All I could see in my mind's eye was Da's face. All his warnings about getting home, and now him sitting at home worried for me.

Now the man was handing me over to another man. I was cradled in his arms, looking up at him, like I was a baby. He looked worried, but he had a kind face.

'What's your name?'

When I tried to speak, I realised how weak I was.

'William Robinson,' I said in a small voice.

He started to run. Every bounce in his arms made my chest and shoulder ache. I knew now that I'd been shot. The pain! It was like a knife stuck in me.

Then he shouted, 'Oi! Stop the cab!'

A motor car pulled up alongside.

'Bring us up to the hospital there. He's been shot. There's been a world of shooting in Croke Park. Don't go down there.'

The driver looked terrified, but he waited as the man placed me gently onto the back seat and got in beside me. I looked at the man.

'Will you tell my da I'm hurt?'

'Of course, lad,' the man said. 'Where is he?'

'Little Britain Street.'

'Right. William Robinson, Little Britain Street. I'll find him, don't worry. But first we need to get you to a hospital.'

I wanted to say thanks, but I couldn't. I hope he knew.

I couldn't even smile.

CHAPTER SEVENTEEN

JERRY

Sitting on the back wall behind the goals as Dublin attacked, Jerry thought the airplane was flying so low his cap might fly off from the wind. He watched the smoke streaming from the flare behind the airplane, bright red against the clear blue sky.

A thick Dublin accent in the crowd below Jerry piped up.

'Is that the Tipperary secret weapon? Bombing us out of it?!'

A wave of laughter swept through the crowd. The airplane veered off towards the city and the game rolled along. Then Jerry heard something else, something no one else in the crowd below him could have spotted yet.

Noises were coming from across to his left, towards the bridge over the canal, just outside Croke Park.

Trucks were stopping on the bridge, while other trucks drove further down the street. He saw Black and Tans jumping out and running towards the bridge. There were Auxiliaries too – he recognised them from his trip to the Castle. In that instant, his mother's words before he left home crashed through his head:

'If you see Black and Tans, I want you back straight away.

'If you see trouble on the road down, I want you back straight away.

'If you get into the ground and something happens, I want you back straight away.'

He saw his mother's face in his mind's eye. Then Dad's face and Mary's. In that moment, he thought of dropping quickly from the wall and slipping through the crowd to make for home.

But he was still sitting motionless on the wall, just staring at the Tans and Auxiliaries. The noise all round him melted away. He was sitting, just looking, like he was frozen in a dream. Some of the soldiers crouched on the bridge. They took up their guns and aimed into the ground. It all happened in an instant, yet everything felt slowed down.

Suddenly, into Jerry's silence came a sharp cracking sound, like a whip. A boy fell from a tree in front of him. Then another crack, almost immediately. Then Jerry O'Leary was falling ...

... falling ...

... falling ...

... until darkness covered everything.

★ ★ ★

It was mid-afternoon at the Castle. Jerry's dad was still there, trapped inside the walls by the soldiers. He walked round the offices and corridors with Lacey, meeting and talking with various people they knew.

They slowly pieced together a picture of the city outside from all the little scraps of information. The trains had been stopped from leaving Dublin. Soldiers and policemen had erected barriers and checkpoints all over the city. They were stopping people and searching them, trying to find any clue to the identities of the killers that morning.

'The hotels all around here are full of people who couldn't get in here,' said one. 'I'd imagine they'll be locked in for the night. No one's safe.'

Then came a flurry of activity. More men appeared to be rushing around, carrying sheaves of paper. Conversations were going on in different offices, rising from soft murmurs to raised voices and panic.

'Oh, good Lord!' Jerome heard one man say on the telephone as he passed a doorway.

'I wonder what's happened,' he whispered to Lacey.

'I'll tell you in a minute,' Lacey replied. He nodded at an officer walking briskly down the corridor towards them, reading over a piece of paper as he approached them.

'Knox,' Lacey said.

'Can't stop,' Knox replied.

'You can spare one second,' Lacey said. 'Just tell me. What is it?'

Knox paused and sighed.

114

'There's been more killing,' he said. 'There was a search operation at the football ground. I don't know its name … there was a football match, or maybe hurling …'

'Croke Park,' Jerome said in a whisper. He felt something grip his chest, like a huge fist squeezing his heart. He thought immediately of Jerry and felt sick.

'Go on,' Lacey said. 'What happened?'

'We don't know,' Knox replied. 'But the Tans and Auxies went there to see what they could find out. They were meant to stop the game and search everyone. But there was firing. They fired back, or they fired first. No one knows exactly …'

Lacey's face darkened.

'Good God man! Who was killed?'

Knox turned pale.

'It's not who,' he said. 'It's how many.'

Jerome was frozen with fear.

'Jerry,' he whispered.

He looked at the other men, eyes widening with terror.

'Jerry!'

He ran off down the corridor and out into the courtyard. He hurried to the great gates at the front of the Castle. The line of soldiers was still there, but the crowds were thinning.

He saw the officer he had met that morning, the one who had pulled him through the people into the Castle.

'You must let me through,' he said.

'I'm sorry, sir,' the officer replied. 'Our orders are to keep everyone inside the walls till further notice.'

'But, my son …' Jerome replied.

The officer looked at him again. 'Your what, sir?'

'My son. He was going to Croke Park. To the football match. Where the police went … the football match …'

The officer looked at the soldier nearest to them and grimaced. Word had already filtered out to the city of the shooting in Croke Park. Many of the people who escaped from the ground had already emerged on the other side of the city. Some were bloodied and wounded. All of them had a story to tell about what they had seen.

'The Tans just started firing!'

'A Tipperary player is dead!'

'There was no escape!'

The officer looked again at Jerry's dad, and gestured for the gate to be opened. 'Get along home, sir. Look after your boy.'

'Thank you,' Jerome said in a whisper. He ran at top speed down the street, looking this way and that for a tram to bring him home.

Back at Croke Park, Jerry lay on the ground as the firing raged on. The officer in charge of the Black and Tans was running to the field, and he shouted at the men to stop shooting when he saw Jerry. He called a spectator to him.

'Take the boy away!' he said.

The spectator looked terrified. Jerry wasn't moving. Was he dead?

'Now!' roared the officer.

The man gathered Jerry in his arms. He seemed lifeless, his face covered in blood. The man lived nearby and decided to carry Jerry to his own house. He hurried out of Croke Park and up the street to his home. He lay Jerry down inside and ran out onto the road looking for help.

An ambulance was approaching the ground. He shouted at the driver as he came close.

'Stop! Help us! We have someone here!'

'I can't,' the driver shouted back. 'They need us for the wounded in the field!

The man kept walking, searching the streets for a way to get Jerry to hospital. He went back to Croke Park and walked inside the gates. The place was quieter now, but still packed with people being lined up and searched.

A man in one corner of the pitch was on his knees, a Black and Tan standing above him, pointing a gun and forcing the man's head to the ground. A woman was lying motionless on the bank in the distance. A line of wounded lay nearby, waiting for ambulances. He saw other shapes lined up alongside each other on the pitch, all dead.

Finally, an ambulance stopped and returned to the house. They placed Jerry down gently into the back of the vehicle.

'Good luck,' said the man as the doors of the ambulance closed.

'God have mercy on him,' he whispered to himself as he went back inside.

CHAPTER EIGHTEEN

JERRY

The ambulance drove towards the Mater Hospital, passing clusters of people on the street. Some were limping and being helped along. Others were holding pieces of cloth against cuts and gashes. Dozens tried to jump aboard the trams rolling past Croke Park.

Other people just stood in the street, watching.

When the ambulance reached the hospital, the orderlies carried Jerry inside. Nurses cleaned the blood from his face as a doctor opened his eyes to examine him.

At home, Jerry's mother looked out the window, watching people on the street below. Crowds were still streaming away from Croke Park, down Blessington Street towards Sackville Street and the city beyond. Mary fretted alongside her.

'Let me go and look for him,' she pleaded. 'Just let me go up the street and see!'

'Mary, I can't let you,' her mother said. 'He'll be home. I know he will. And if he's not, your father will know what to do. Look out there. It's too dangerous. You can't go out into that.'

But her heart was already quietly breaking. She wanted to drop everything and run outside to find Jerry, to hold him close and bring him home. She didn't know about the firing in Croke Park, but she heard shots pinging like fire crackers now and saw the look on people's faces as they hurried past her window.

She thought of Jerry, but she had to think of Mary too. And what would their father do? She had to protect them all and pray that Jerry was somewhere in the crowd, hurrying home.

Time passed. The early winter darkness began to fall on the city. The crowds of people hurrying past their door became a stream, then a trickle. Then, there was silence.

Mary looked to her mother, sitting in a corner, lost in her thoughts.

'Ma, please,' she said again. 'Let me go.'

Her mother looked out the window. The light was fading. The bright sunshine that had warmed them all day had been chased away by the cold. Where was Jerry? Where was Jerome? She looked at Mary, feeling tears coming to her eyes.

'You can go,' she said. 'But be back within the hour. If you see soldiers, go the other way. If you see police, look away. If you find your father, come home with him.'

She stood up and crossed the room and took Mary in her arms, hugging her tightly.

'We don't know what has happened,' she said. 'For now, we only have each other. Be careful, Mary. Just be careful.'

Mary forced a smile. 'It'll be alright, Ma,' she said. 'Jerry is probably at someone's house. I know where to go.'

But she didn't really. Her mother followed her out of the room to the landing, and Mary ran downstairs and opened the front door. She turned and looked back. In that moment, her mother looked so small and frail. The worry was sucking the life from her.

'I'll be back soon, Ma,' Mary said, and closed the door.

The street outside was dotted with people rushing along, but strangely quiet. No one spoke. She was halfway to Croke Park when a shrunken old man with craggy features and dressed in ragged clothes stopped her on the street.

'Don't go near that place,' he said, pointing towards the field. 'They've shot them all, girleen. Shot them all!'

Mary was startled, but she kept walking. Police trucks wailed past, filled with Black and Tans. The sky was getting darker. She continued along Jones' Road, where the bridge crossed the canal and the houses gathered around Croke Park. Ambulances drove by, stopping at houses to collect the wounded.

Could Jerry be in one of those houses?

She stopped at one.

'Excuse me,' she said to a man helping to carry a man on a stretcher from his home. 'Have you seen any young boys about here? Ten years old? Brown hair?'

The man turned to her as they loaded the stretcher into the ambulance.

'Sure, the place was full of little fellas earlier,' he said. 'But there was none in my house.'

She heard a shot ring out, further up the street. It startled her.

'Go on home,' said the man. 'The lad you're looking for, he's probably somewhere in the city by now.'

Mary was too frightened to speak. She ran along the street, looking down alleys and in front windows for any sign of Jerry. This is useless, she thought.

Then she heard a familiar voice.

'Mary!'

Jerome had spotted Mary up the street, her eyes read from tears and the cold.

'Da!'

He ran to her and hugged her tightly.

'You go home, Mary,' said Jerome. 'I'll talk to the police and see what I can find out. Don't worry, pet, he'll be home. He's a rascal, but he's clever enough to get away from this.'

Jerome smiled kindly. For the first time all afternoon, Mary felt some hope.

'Alright, Da,' she said. 'I'll tell Ma I found you.'

'Do that, pet,' he replied, squeezing her hand. 'Go on now.'

Mary wiped the tears from her eyes and turned for home. Jerome walked on towards Croke Park. Just before the canal bridge where the police had fired from before, he saw an officer of the Dublin Metropolitan Police on patrol.

'Look here, sir!' cried Jerome, flashing his pass from the Castle.

The policeman looked startled.

'Sir, get on home, please. It's not safe here.'

'I'm looking for my son,' he replied. 'Ten years old, brown hair. Did you see anyone like that in the field?'

'I wasn't in the field, sir,' said the policeman. 'But you'll never find him here. All the dead and wounded are gone to the hospitals now. And sure, most of them jumped on trams to get away.'

The policeman looked back up the street towards the last convoys of Black and Tans, still lingering around Croke Park, and turned again to Jerome.

'Please, sir,' he said, 'I'm sure you're worried, but they're in a wretched mood now. They killed people here in cold blood. It was pure chaos. In all my years I've never seen the like. I did see one boy that was hurt, behind me by the tree below, sir, but he looked older. Try the hospitals, sir. But get away from here now.'

Jerome was pale with worry. He nodded to the policeman. 'Thank you,' he croaked.

He walked up the road to the Drumcondra Hospital, where William Robinson lay, waiting for his father and mother to come. The Jervis Street Hospital, where many of the dead were taken, was further into the city. The Mater Hospital was next nearest.

Jerome set off on foot. It was dark now. He could see search-lights beaming out from the centre of the city, strafing the sky overhead. The streets were quiet, save for the occasional crack of a gunshot.

Outside the Mater Hospital, scores of people were gathered. Some were murmuring together in prayer. Old women in dark shawls gathered together, talking in low voices. A handful of soldiers stood nearby, ready to step in if the mood turned ugly. A few more stood guard at the entrance, watching the crowd outside waiting for news.

Jerome nudged his way through the mass of people, showed his pass and slipped into the entrance hall. He went to the desk, where an agitated nurse sat, flicking through a stack of files. She looked up and fixed him with a stare.

'Yes?'

'I'm looking for a boy, Jerry O'Leary. He might have come from Croke Park. Ten years old, brown hai–'

The nurse frowned.

'So many people came to the hospital without any details,' she said. 'Some were unconscious and couldn't speak. Are you the father?'

'Yes.'

She pointed to a spot down the corridor behind him.

'Go there. Second ward on the left. There are children there.'

'Thank you,' said Jerome, as the nurse returned to her files.

He walked quickly down the corridor. The sick feeling in the pit of his stomach that had been there since morning was growing heavier. He could feel it rising towards his throat. His arms and legs were quivering with fear. All he wanted was to see Jerry and hold him, to bring him home.

He reached the ward and looked inside. Children were lying in two rows of beds along the walls. A couple sat on chairs. A kindly nurse came to greet him.

'Can I help you?'

'Yes, I'm looking for my son, Jerry O'Leary. He might have been brought from Croke Park, I don't know. He hasn't come home and we don't know where to look, and ...'

He was talking so quickly he was scarcely making any sense.

'That's alright, sir,' the nurse replied. 'Just calm down and tell me what he looked like. There is no Jerry O'Leary on this ward, but we can find him if he's here.'

'Sorry,' said Jerome. 'Thank you. He's ten years of age, small with brown hair. He would have been wearing a dark, heavy coat. As I say, he might not be here. We don't know where he went, but he was at Croke Park ...'

'Okay,' said the nurse. 'Can you just hang on one minute please? Just wait here in the corridor.'

She walked quickly towards a desk at the end of the corridor. Jerome watched her speaking quietly to another nurse. Both of them looked back in his direction. The nurse then walked back and took him by the arm.

'Please, sir, come with me.'

They walked silently down the corridor and around the corner, then down some steps into a darker, windowless part of the hospital.

'Where are we going?' asked Jerome.

The nurse didn't answer immediately. They came to a door.

'I'm afraid …' the nurse paused and looked into his eyes. 'Sir, I'm afraid many of the wounded were brought here. Some are still alive. Some are not. There is a boy here. I do not know if he is your boy, but you are the first person to come looking for someone who looks like him.'

Jerome could feel that sick sensation boiling inside him. His skin felt hot and itchy. Tears were gathering behind his eyes. He nodded and took a deep breath.

'He is in this room. If you know him, please tell us.'

The nurse opened the door. The room was coloured pale in the light that shone above a small boy lying on a bed. His skin was soft white. His face was still and perfect, apart from a red mark on his forehead.

Jerome nodded. This was his son. His shoulders began to shake as tears streamed down his cheeks. He sobbed quietly, holding the top of the bed. He ran his hand along the side of Jerry's cold cheek.

'My boy,' he whispered. 'Oh, my precious boy.'

CHAPTER NINETEEN

BILLY

Charlie Daly shifted in his armchair and paused to take a sip of tea. A million feelings were rushing up inside him, like a wave racing towards the shore.

'Charlie, what did you know about Bloody Sunday and the spies that had been killed, going down to Billy Scott's house?'

'Sure, I knew very little. You'd have heard of the shootings and there was a few checkpoints in the town. No cars were on the road and the trains were shut down. So the town was quiet, but around Croke Park on a big day, ah sure, it was packed.'

'Did people not want to stay away?'

'Not by the looks of things! I mean, there was 15,000 people there. It was a huge crowd. And Croke Park was very different to what you'd see now.'

'How so?'

'Ah well, you need to imagine the place in your mind. Take down all the big stands and Hill 16, the terrace that's there now, and imagine a big, broad sports field. At the north end, where Hill 16 is now, there was the wall of the railway embankment, then some flat land behind the goals and a sort of mound in the top right-hand-corner. That was called Hill 60 then – it was only called Hill 16 years later, in honour of the 1916 Rising and that. Hill 60 was about a battle during the First World War, where a lot of Irish men died.

'Back then, you had a long bank stretching down the east side, where the Cusack Stand is now. There was a tall wall at the back, six or seven feet high, but that dropped way down into the sports grounds owned by Belvedere College. That's the school nearby. Twenty feet drop or so I'd say.

'Along the south side was a low bank with a wall, and the Royal Canal running along the back there. Then on the west side, where the big Hogan Stand is now, that was one long sort of grandstand with a pavilion underneath. That's where the dressing rooms were and all. There was an entrance gate in the middle there, and some trees down in the corner by the canal bridge.

'It was all very hemmed in compared to now. You go to Croke Park now and it's all wide-open streets and space around the whole place. But back then, houses and back gardens came right up to the ground. It was all little alleys around it.'

'Did you call to Billy's house?'

'Yes, I got to Fitzroy Avenue through the crowd. It was late enough, but the game was delayed and he lived so close to the pitch he could wait for me. I remember his ma and da were there. And his grandfather. I just called in, I don't think I even got beyond the hall of the house and he was down the stairs, ready to go. Pure excitement. It was a great day out, going to Croke Park.'

'What did you talk about on the way?'

'Ach, probably nothing. We'd only have been walking maybe five minutes. School maybe? The size of the crowd? I do remember the little pink tickets on the tables of the ticket sellers by the turnstiles. They were bright pink that day. It was a funny splash of colour amongst all those dark coats.

'We got inside the ground, down by the canal wall and found a spot where we could see through the people. I remember that the teams were ready but the game was late starting, because of the crowd. And I remember the plane flying over and letting off a flare. But we had no idea what was coming. No idea.'

'What did you and Billy do when the firing started?'

'I remember we tried to run. We were close enough to an exit, but the police were coming in that way and everyone was running away from them, so we kind of got caught.

'It's odd, parts of it almost went in slow motion. People were just running everywhere, screaming. People were climbing the wall, trying to get out by the canal. The policemen were just firing at anyone running away.

'I saw one fella, he was shooting a revolver from his hip, like a cowboy in the films or something. There was these sparks way up the other end of the ground; like little fireworks they were. I only realised after that those were bullets, bouncing off the walls.'

'Did you see anyone killed?'

'I do remember Mick Hogan, the Tipperary player. I didn't see him shot, but when we were trying to get out, I just glanced and saw him lying on the ground and another man kneeling with him. Then that man fell. There was a little boy by the wall as well. But our only thought was just trying to escape.'

'And what happened to Billy?'

'Well, we were together, but then the crowd sort of got in between us and swept him away. I lost him. That's what happened. I lost him.

'I eventually got out, through the garden of a house. I got onto Jones' Road outside and everyone was just running. So I ran. I ran and ran and ran and I never stopped till I was so far from Croke Park I couldn't see it any more.'

'When did you hear what had happened to Billy?'

'Honest to God, I don't know. I'd gotten away, but he wasn't with me. When I got my breath back, I tried to go back to find him, but there was so many people. Some of them were covered in blood. Some were limping or holding an arm or their face after being hurt. I saw priests rushing back towards the pitch, and there was soldiers everywhere.

'I was only a child. You know, we felt like such grown-ups, going to that match. But then something like that happens and all you want is to get home safe. But I heard the story afterwards.'

'What was the story?'

'Sure, it was desperate. Just desperate. The firing didn't last that long, not even a couple of minutes, but the police and soldiers were around Croke Park for ages after, searching people and taking pot shots.

'Eventually, people started coming out of their houses. The Scotts only lived across the road from Croke Park, so they'd have heard all the firing and seen all the people running for their lives. And you can only imagine the worry when Billy and me didn't come home.

'Billy's da went looking for him. Someone along the way told him to go up to St James's Avenue, the street that runs along the back of Hill 16 now, and go to this lady's house. So he did, and the lady told him the whole story.'

'What did she say?'

'It's hard to talk about this, so I'm sorry ... She told him that Billy had been brought to the house by some men, who sheltered in the house with him. He had been hit in the chest ... we found out later it was a bullet that had ricocheted, off a wall or something.

'He was in terrible pain, the woman told his da. They put him on a table and the lady and her daughter knelt and said some prayers. He needed water, but no one could go to the tap outside, because the bullets were still flying and the police were raiding houses and pulling people out everywhere.

'So they just knelt and they prayed. Billy was able to answer some of them. "Pray for me," the lady said he told them.'

'When did he die?'

'He held on for forty-five minutes, moaning and gasping for air. Then he died. That was it.'

'I'm sorry to make you tell that story again. Is it hard?'

'It's just the pure sadness of it. He was only a boy. The two of us were just boys. I lost my friend. His ma and da lost their son. His grandad was heartbroken. After he died, the military came to the house and took his body outside.

They left him on the street for an ambulance to take away. Can you imagine? The woman had to go out with a blanket to cover him.'

'How was Billy's father? Did you ever hear?'

'We did. Sure, he was like any da. He couldn't believe his son was dead. He didn't want to. When the lady told him the whole story, he still asked, was she totally sure the boy was Billy? His Billy?

'Then she handed him Billy's glasses and his tiepin. And that was it. He knew Billy was gone.'

CHAPTER TWENTY

PERRY

We weren't in the cab very long once we took off from Croke Park. The hospital was only up the road, but the crowds were so thick it was hard to get going.

So the car was shunting forwards, then stopping suddenly. Every jerk was pure agony. I moaned with the pain sometimes, even though I tried my best to stay quiet. The man looking after me tried to move me around on the seat to make me comfortable, but there was no way.

'Just stay calm, son,' he'd say every few minutes. 'We're nearly there now.'

I knew he meant well, but it was so sore. Finally we stopped. The man carefully lifted me from the back seat and carried me inside. Soon I was on a trolley being wheeled somewhere. I couldn't open my eyes now, but I could hear voices.

'Is it okay if I leave him here? I need to find his mother and father.'

'Sir, if you could just wait a short while. Do you know this boy?'

'I don't. He was handed to me by a Tan to bring away. He's been asking for his da; all I want is to find his parents.'

'Could you just sit with him a few minutes while we find someone to examine him, sir? He needs that now more than he needs his mother or father. Just a few minutes.'

I could hear him talking to me.

'It's okay, William, I'll be going soon. It's nearly five o'clock. They'll surely let me away into town. Just stay with us. Can you hear me, William?

'William?'

Everything was quiet. Had I passed out? Was I asleep? Then I felt the cold sensation of a stethoscope on my chest. My breathing was shallow. I was gasping. I felt so weak. Any time I tried to move an arm or a leg, it felt like I was made of lead.

I felt someone probing around the place where the bullet went through my chest and out my shoulder. I heard the doctor say, 'He's very lucky to be alive, this boy. I don't know how long he can last, but we'll do our best.'

Then everything was muffled, like someone had put their hands over my ears. I could smell the hospital. I could feel cold air seeping across from an open window some-where nearby, brushing against my ear. I heard the man's voice again.

'Doctor, before he passed out, this boy asked me to find his father and bring him here. Now that you have his name and you've seen his condition, can I leave to find him?'

'Yes, of course,' said the doctor. 'But leave your name with the nurse at the desk. If anything happens, you'll have to be the first person we contact.'

'Thank you, doctor,' The man said. Then I felt his breath against my ear.

'Hang in there, William,' he said. 'Your da will be here really soon. I'll be in Little Britain Street in no time. I'll say a prayer.'

I felt the cold air again. He was gone. It was such a strange sensation, once I knew he was gone looking for my da, how my whole body relaxed. The pain ebbed away a little bit. I could feel myself being rolled along again, into a room where it went all quiet. I felt then like I was drifting off to sleep.

I don't know how long had passed before I heard a voice somewhere outside the room.

'Where's my boy? Where's my boy?!'

The door opened. I heard sobs, then I felt my da's hand gripping my hand, his fingers locked into mine. I could smell home from him. I shifted my fingers a little.

'He moved, doctor! See that?'

'Mr Robinson, he is very weak. We're doing what we can, but he is very weak. Perhaps we could speak outside.'

I already had a good idea what the doctor was telling him. I could feel my body getting lighter. It was as if I was carrying a pile of heavy bags, and then someone started taking them away, one at a time.

My breathing was slowing down. I knew what was happening, but hearing my father's voice, then my mother's, I felt peaceful.

Time passed. Hours, days. I heard people come and go, my father's voice telling them I was poorly and what had happened. I heard the voice of the man who had brought me to hospital and my father and mother thanking him, blessing him.

Sometimes I felt small surges of energy inside myself. I tried to grab hold of them, hoping they might pull me out of this sleep. But I couldn't open my eyes.

The voices gradually became more distant.

Then there was no sound at all.

The pain in my chest started to ebb away, until there was no pain at all.

The lightness in my body seemed to lift me away from all those things.

Away to somewhere else.

CHAPTER TWENTY-ONE

BILLY

Charlie produced an envelope, and very carefully took out a half-dozen delicate newspaper cuttings, all yellowed from age.

'These are newspaper articles from the days straight after Bloody Sunday. My father kept these, because he knew they were important.

'You can look through them if you like. Everyone was told at the time that the IRA had started the firing, shooting at the police outside the ground. The British were certain about that. You'll see in the articles there, they claimed they found lots of guns on the field and around Croke Park. But sure, they found nothing in reality. None of it was true.

'All I know is, I saw that airplane, and then the firing started. And that was it.'

'Did people believe them?'

'Not really, but most people didn't talk about it all

that much. There were special inquiries afterwards and lots of people who were there were interviewed, but we never heard much back. The British insisted that the IRA started it, but anyone in the ground that day said the firing started with the Tans out on the bridge.'

'Was there a story about Billy though?'

'Yes. I was just coming to that. See, in the week afterwards, there was all sorts of commotion in Britain about Bloody Sunday. People were upset at the spies getting killed, and all of them got heros' funerals. And there were lots of questions from politicians in the House of Commons. There was even a fight! One of the Irish MPs was asking after the people hurt in Croke Park and another MP grabbed him.

'But there was also a question about Billy. See, I never saw him after the shooting started, but he got hit in the chest. The wound was so bad, the papers thought he'd been stabbed. Bayoneted, with the knife the soldiers could attach to the top of their guns, you know?

'A lady MP, Nancy Astor, asked if Billy had been bayoneted. She was told he hadn't been, but that was how people were thinking.

'And there's an article here about when his Da found him ... I might read this out if that's alright? So it's recorded on the tape then:

A little boy named John Wm Scott (Billie), aged 14, was taken into a house in James Avenue, Clonliffe Road, suffering from what appeared to be a bayonet wound to the chest, and he died in the house, his body being afterwards taken to the Mater Hospital by the military.

His father, John Scott, resides at 15 Fitzroy Avenue, and told a *Freeman's Journal* reporter that the boy who was killed was his eldest child and had been attending Saint Patrick's School, Drumcondra. The boy had his dinner on Sunday and then hurried off to the match with a playmate, a little fellow named Daly. Hearing that a boy had been killed and was lying in a house at James's Avenue, the father proceeded there, but found that the body had been taken away by the military. The lady who occupies the house showed him the glasses and tie-pin belonging to the boy, however, and he recognised them as his son's. The father afterwards identified the body. There was a wound across the left breast, which apparently had been caused by a bullet.

Mrs Colman, 37 James's Avenue, told our representative that when young Scott was carried into her house he was bleeding from the chest and seemed to be in great pain. A number of men had sought shelter in her house and in other houses in the avenue. The little boy was placed on a table. Mrs Colman and her two girls knelt down by his side and said some prayers, and the poor boy made the responses. All the time the rattle of shots was heard outside, some being fired up the Avenue, and they were unable to get out for a drink of water for the dying child. He was suffering greatly and moaning a lot, and he died about three-quarters of an hour after he was brought in.

Subsequently the military entered the house and took the body outside. It was lying in the avenue for some time, covered by a blanket which Mrs Colman had placed over it, and was then taken away by the military.'

'It's so sad, Charlie.,

'Sure it's so sad. I'm an old man now, but I remember that day and I remember my friend. We were only boys that went to a match, and Billy never came home.'

'And what happened to you?'

'I just ran until I got home. And I remember my Ma hadn't heard what had gone on … sure, there was no phones or television back then. Not even the radio. So I told her the story, about going to the game with Billy and how he had gotten lost in the crowd – I didn't know he was dead yet – and she just gathered me up in the tightest … the tightest, most frightened hug you can imagine. I can still feel her arms around me that evening, like she'd never let me go.

'Then my da landed in. He looked awful worried until he saw me in the house, saw that I was okay.'

'And how did you find out about Billy?'

'It was late that night. I was in bed and someone came to the door. It might have been a priest, I don't know. And my ma came in, I remember, and whispered to see if I was awake. Sure, every time I closed my eyes, all I saw was Billy and I heard the sound of the guns in my head.

'I sat up in the bed and she sat down and told me. "Billy was shot," she said. "Lord have mercy on him."'

'How did that make you feel?'

'I didn't know what to do, but my ma could see in my eyes what I felt. Mothers always know what their children are feeling. She just held me for what felt like the longest time. I was numb, in shock really. I remember lying back on my pillow, and she said good night, that we'd say prayers for Billy in the morning and not to worry about school.

'When the door closed, I closed my eyes and I saw Billy again. He was laughing and messing like we always did, teasing me and I having a crack back at him. And now, my friend was gone.

'I started to cry then, just quietly to myself. And I cried for a long time that night. You know, all the times I've thought about Billy since that day, when I'm alone by myself, I've not really stopped crying for him since.'

CHAPTER
TWENTY-TWO

JERRY

The silence in the house on Sunday evening was terrible. Mary sat on a chair at the table, her hands wrapped around her legs, her knees gathered up beneath her chin. She looked very small.

Jerry's mother sat on her armchair opposite Mary, staring at the floor. The silence was only broken by the odd whispered prayer and the sounds of people on the street below.

It was dark when the front door creaked open and closed gently. Jerome's footsteps up the stairs were slow, almost silent. Mam ran out to the landing. Mary stayed in the sitting room, holding herself tightly. She heard her dad talking quietly. Then her mam begin to wail. She knew then.

Jerome came in and looked across at Mary. She had held her tears all the way home from Croke Park and tried to stay calm when telling her mam what she knew: that she couldn't find Jerry, and that Dad was gone to the hospitals to find him.

But now, seeing Dad, his eyes sad and glassy from the tears he had cried on the way home, she began to cry too. He went to her and lifted her off the chair, holding Mary close to him with a hug she wished could last forever.

'It's alright, Mary,' he whispered. 'It's alright. Let it go. Let the tears out.'

Mam was sitting on the edge of her chair, staring blankly. She began to talk, slowly at first but then quickly.

'We'll need to contact your mother and father, Jerome,' she said. 'And mine.

'And the priest.

'And the hospital.

'Where will we have the Mass?

'What about a place to bury him?'

She looked at Dad, almost in tears.

'Where will we bury him?'

Dad reached his hand across the room, and grabbed his wife by the wrist, pulling her across to him and Mary. He took them both in his arms and hugged them tightly.

'Shush now,' he said softly. 'Cry your tears for our boy first. All of us must think of Jerry now, think of him and hold him close. We'll let the world in tomorrow.'

They sat there for what seemed like forever, in the shadows cast by the half-light of an oil lamp, clinging to each other, wishing away tomorrow, hoping it would never come.

None of them slept that night. Mary tossed and turned in her bed. She sensed her mother nearby, sobbing and sitting on the edge of the bed, touching Jerry's books and toys, running her hand across his clothes in the little set of drawers.

The sound of gunshots from across the city echoed down their street. Jerome heard the following day that another boy and an old man had been killed by the Army. They had been trying to clear people while the police made arrests in some houses on the other side of Sackville Street.

Jerome left early for the hospital again and sent telegrams to some relatives down the country. Then he went to see Canon Downing, the unsinkable old parish priest, to ask if he could say Jerry's funeral Mass.

'I can and I will,' he said. 'How are you? How is the family?'

Jerome was nervous and agitated.

'It doesn't feel real, Father,' he replied. 'But we'll be fine. With the grace of God.'

'The love of the Lord is all round you now,' Canon Downing said, putting his hand on Jerome's shoulder. 'Stay close and look after each other. We all share in your grief now.'

Dad nodded and headed home. In the afternoon, a newspaper man called to the door, looking for a picture of Jerry for the following day's newspapers. 'Yes, of course,' said Mam, scarcely realising what they were asking for. She returned with a small picture of Jerry, sitting on a chair in a white jersey, his hair combed neatly forward. He was maybe eight or nine.

'Thank you, ma'am,' he said. 'I'll have it back to you tomorrow.'

She wept again when the newspaper man was gone.

That evening, a Dublin Metropolitan Police constable called to the house. Jerome answered the door.

'Mr O'Leary?'

'Yes.'

'I was sorry to hear of your boy, sir. I have instructions from the military on the funeral arrangements.'

Dad looked confused. What possible business of theirs was this?

'The authorities have ruled that all funerals will only be attended by close family and friends. No flags or banners are permitted. No speeches and no political statements will be allowed.'

The constable looked nervously at Jerome. 'I'm sorry, sir. I don't mean to bring this sort of news to you, but I'm obliged to let you kno—'

'It's alright, Constable,' Jerome interrupted. 'It's alright. Thank you. We have no intention of doing anything other than burying our boy in peace and quiet.'

The constable's face relaxed a little.

'I understand, sir. These are terrible times. Bless his soul, sir. I'll leave you be.'

The constable left, and Jerome closed the door. He felt the same pang he often got when he saw the Black and Tans and Auxiliaries in the Castle laughing and joking, dragging a suspect across the courtyard for interrogation.

'This is how it is,' he thought. 'This is how it must be.'

BILLY

'Charlie, do you remember much about Billy's funeral?'

'Well, before that, I'll tell you what I remember very well. That was the story of Billy being found. You remember I told you about his da calling to Mrs Colman's house? And she giving him Billy's glasses and tiepin?'

'Yes?'

'Well, he went home to tell everyone the news. Billy's mother took weak. She couldn't bear it. The crying and the wailing, the neighbours said you could hear it echoing way down the street.

'People called to see what was wrong, and they left devastated by the news. Then Billy's da went to the hospital to identify him. Even that was dangerous enough stuff. The Black and Tans were still around Croke Park that evening. One fella had gotten shot when he was leaving the ground, so no one felt safe. Everyone just got away home and locked their doors. We all feared the worst.

'But he went and found Billy and came home. The newspaper people were calling then, the following day. I remember Billy's picture in the paper and my da reading out the story of how he was found. My own mother was so upset when he was reading, she told him to stop. The house went very quiet that day. I've never forgotten it.'

'And did you go to the funeral?'

'Ah, we were there of course. The whole school was there. We were all in our uniforms in the church. I remember feeling weirdly empty. It was unreal.

'When you're fourteen, you don't expect anyone to die that's your age, especially not your friend. I just kept thinking of the day and the bit of fun we had. And I wanted to freeze the memories so I wouldn't forget him. I wanted to hold onto his voice so I could always hear him. That's what I tried to do then, I remember that well.

'He was gone, but I didn't want to lose him.

'But no one really said much about what happened. We said prayers for Billy and offered up his soul to the Lord. Then we got on with life. We went back to school. That was as good as we could do. But I never forgot him.'

'Was there a big crowd at the funeral?'

'Well, you see, the police were frightened that the IRA or someone would turn up and make a show out of it for themselves. So they put all these limits on the families about who could go. But people turned up. All we wanted to do was say goodbye to Billy.

'They buried him in the middle of the old cemetery in Glasnevin. It's shaded by a line of trees. You can see Daniel O'Connell's round tower from where he is. I remember that day there was lots of people around, because a few more of the people who died in Croke Park were also buried that day. Billy was buried in the morning, then other people came. I remember the big cortege for the lady who died, Jane Boyle. She was to be married the following week. I recall someone saying that she was buried in her wedding dress. That was the way it was, little sad stories connected to all these people.'

'And how was Billy's family? How was his mother?'

'Ah, poor Mary was so sad, I don't know if she even went to the funeral. I remember his da was there, and his grandad. They were at the top of the church and they walked behind the coffin. I've sometimes wondered how his grandad felt about it all. Remember, this was a man who had fought for King and country. He was an English man, who raised his family in Ireland.

'Now his grandson had been killed at a football match. Was he killed by the IRA shooting at the police, like the government said? Or was he killed by the Black and

Tans? It was in all the papers, all sorts of accounts of what had happened, terrible stories of people being injured, people jumping on trams outside Croke Park to escape, wounded and covered in blood.

'There were stories about bullets pinging off the walls, making little sparks. All I remember was the terrible push of the crowd when we were all trying to escape, and breathing in this fresh blast of air when I was outside on the road, and then running for home.

'All Mr Chapman knew for certain was that his grandson was gone and that his daughter – Billy's ma – was back home not able to even come to the funeral. She wasn't able to let Billy go. Not then, not ever. None of them ever did.'

PERRY

They buried me on the Friday in Glasnevin Cemetery. It's not far from Croke Park, just a little further to the north. There's a big round tower here, marking the spot where Daniel O'Connell is buried. It's a really big place, with rows and rows of graves.

My grave is in a quiet part of the cemetery, across from the main bit where they buried all the famous people. The day of my funeral? Sure, you can imagine. I was only a boy. The sadness was desperate. The Mass was in Halston Street church, just across from where I lived. All the friends were there, and family, neighbours, people from the fruit markets and lots of people who knew my ma and da up and down the years.

It reminded me of my uncle William's funeral. I remembered looking at his boys and girls that day, and how empty their ma looked behind her eyes. And no one there knew where to look or what to say.

It was the same at my funeral. They just said their prayers and whispered small sympathies to my ma and da.

'So sorry for your trouble.'

'May the Lord have mercy on his little soul.'

'He's with the angels now, looking down on youse.'

Sure, what do you say? For a family to lose two people shot in barely a month? The shock was terrible. Everyone was still numb and disbelieving. My da did most of the talking those few days to people. My ma went quiet. She cried and cried; her eyes had red circles she cried so much.

The sun was shining the day they buried me. The cemetery was quiet. The police told my family: no flags and no banners about politics or the IRA or anything else. No one firing gunshots over the grave and all that. Only family and very close friends were allowed. My da got mad with them when they called to him.

'Sure, what would we want with all that?' he told them. 'Can you not just leave us bury our boy in peace!'

At the same time we were being buried, the spies that the IRA shot were being carried down the quays to a boat and taken to England for their funerals. Everyone on the street had to take their hats off as they passed. Anyone who didn't got their hat thrown into the Liffey. Imagine that.

'And we're barely allowed come up here to pray for a little boy?' said one fella from the markets at my funeral. 'There's something wrong with the world when it comes to this.'

When the funeral was over, everyone went home and time carried on; everyone put their sadness aside to concentrate on the living. I don't think anyone ever forgot about me – not my own family anyway. When my mother died, we got a headstone. That was thirty-two years later, in 1952. She had bronchitis. Her heart gave out in the end.

But what a gravestone! It was made from Carrara marble. Now, I didn't know anything about this of course, but I've heard people say that Carrara marble was used to build the Pantheon in Rome. And the sculpture of David by Michelangelo, which is very famous it seems.

I don't know how my crowd got that marble, but it was beautiful and white and glowed when it was clean. And when the gravestone was eventually put in place, they carved my name on it for everyone to remember me by. Here's what it says:

IHS

in loving memory of our dear mother

BRIDGET ROBINSON

died 14th Oct. 1952

our dear brother WILLIAM

grand mother MARIA DWAN

grand father JOSEPH DWAN

our uncle EDWARD DWAN

R. I. P.

It was tragic, everyone said. Such a young boy, killed at a football match. Just tragic.

It was.

CHAPTER
TWENTY-THREE

JERRY

Time passed. Days turned into nights. Nights gave way to more days. Days became weeks and eventually months. Jerry's dad returned to the Castle to work. Mary returned to school, where people said little about Jerry. Her mother held her grief close and turned to the simple rituals of the house: cleaning

and cooking

and washing

and sewing

and mending.

Trying to find the face of God and his grace in her work, trying to find cracks of light in the sadness hanging over every passing day.

Summer came. The Castle buzzed with news. The fighting since Bloody Sunday had turned more ferocious. The IRA had been energised by the killing of so many spies that morning; the British struck back with brutality.

It was June, and Jerry's dad was walking near home, when three men in caps emerged on the street. They produced guns and started firing at him.

Jerome ran, but the sharp pain of a bullet knocked him to the ground. His mind was ablaze with terror. He pulled himself up and ran again. The firing started again.

Who were these people?

He clambered up a set of steps and through an open doorway. A man and a young girl were standing there, and they hurried him inside. Looked back, he got a glimpse of one gunman.

He knew him. It was Durnin, their neighbour.

IRA.

Jerome was ushered into a living room and given a chair. The man of the house looked concerned.

'I'm a doctor,' he said. 'Whelan. Where were you hit?'

Blood seeped out through Jerome's clothes. The doctor pressed around the wound. Jerome winced.

'I am shot,' he said. 'My God, I have done nothing to anybody.'

'It's a flesh wound,' the doctor said. 'You'll be fine, but we need to get you to hospital.'

He turned to the girl. 'Daughter, be careful. Look out the window and see who's there. Is there a motor car or maybe some police?'

The girl peeked out a corner of the window. Two policemen were talking to people on the street. The people were pointing at her house.

In a few moments, the police were at the door.

'Is the gentleman alright?'

'He will be,' replied the doctor. 'But he needs to get to hospital.'

They flagged down a car and carried Jerome down the steps. A crowd had gathered.

'Go on, clear off!' shouted a policeman. He ran around the car and jumped into the front seat beside the driver. 'Get this man to the Mater Hospital. Quickly!'

Days passed and Jerome eventually recovered. When Mary and her mother visited, they talked a little, never a lot. Sometimes the silence between them went on for what seemed like hours, none of them able to find the right words.

'They thought I was a spy,' he would tell them. 'God save us. A spy.'

All of them wondered what the future might bring. 'Are we staying or going, Ma?' Mary would ask at home. Her mother would shake her head.

'Now is not the time, Mary. Let your father come home and we will talk then.'

One day, at the hospital, Jerome looked at them both seriously and pulled himself upright in bed.

'I'm feeling stronger now,' he said. 'The doctor has said I'm almost ready to come home. I received word the Castle will give me some money as compensation. Maybe £700.'

Mary Jane smiled. 'That's good news, Jerome.'

'But we must make decisions now,' he said. 'I have had time to think. Sure, I haven't been able to do anything else! How can we call this place our home anymore? My life was almost taken by one of our neighbours. We cannot walk the streets without talk following us. Lies and rumours about me.'

'We could go back to Cork,' Mary Jane said. 'Or Limerick? Life was always good there.'

Jerome lowered his voice to a whisper.

'The IRA are everywhere,' he said. 'All they need is a word and my life is in danger again. I cannot risk leaving you and Mary alone. We have already lost Jerry …'

His voice began to break. He looked away as the tears came.

'Jerome, dear,' Mary Jane said. 'You must not carry that guilt. What happened to Jerry was not your fault. We carry that sadness together, all of us. From now till eternity. Whatever we do, whatever life we live, we will live it together.'

She squeezed his hand hard. Jerome wiped the tears from his eyes and cheeks and took a breath.

'Look at our lives' he said. 'Trapped in two rooms at the top of a house, constantly in fear of our safety. What kind of life is that? What kind of life is it for Mary?'

He looked sternly at them both.

'We must leave.'

Mary's eyes welled with tears. Her father held her hand.

'Mary, dear. There is nothing here for us. Our boy is gone. I could have been killed. We must take care of each other now. And this is no safe place for us anymore.'

He turned to her mother.

'Make plans for London,' he said. 'As soon as the money comes through and I'm well, we will leave.'

'Yes,' she replied quietly.

The silence returned again. They knew what leaving would mean. They might never return to Dublin. Who would remember Jerry? Who would place flowers on his grave and think of him every late November and say a prayer?

But how could they stay, living under these clouds of fear and sadness, terrified every day?

The silence was finally punctured by Mary. She tightened her grip on her father's hand.

'We have no choice,' she said. 'I know we have no choice.'

BILLY

'Charlie, when it was all over and years passed, did you find it hard to live with the memories?'

'Sometimes. Sometimes it was hard to sleep. I remember going back to school. That was hard. It was a different time, you see. People didn't talk about what was bothering them. If you felt sad, you swallowed it down and got on with it.'

'And did you feel sad?'

'Of course! Sure, I'd lost my friend. You'd miss calling to the house and having fun going around the streets and in school. Imagine if your best friend was gone?

'But after Bloody Sunday, it felt like someone threw a big cover over the whole thing, like a big blanket. The authorities had an inquiry and they decided that the IRA had fired at the police first, from inside Croke Park. That's what had started the shooting, they said. No one believed that, but there wasn't a word said. Again, people just wanted to get on.'

'Do you visit Billy's grave?'

'The odd time, maybe in November, around the time of Bloody Sunday. Tipperary played Dublin in matches for years in Croke Park to mark the anniversary. I went to a few of those. But some years, it was too hard.

'When you get to my age, all you have is memories. Your friends are gone. All the people you knew are leaving you. And then you think of Billy, taken away at fourteen. We'd have known a few others as well who got hurt or killed in the troubles down the years after that. So much loss … so much loss.'

PERRY

So we're all here now in this place, in this cemetery, with all its stories and its ghosts. You'd often hear people visiting graves down the years say the same thing: 'Ah, death. Sure, 'tis the great leveller.'

What do they mean? I suppose it's like everyone might have ideas about themselves when they're alive.

Some people are rich.

Some are poor.

Some are soldiers.

Some are IRA men.

Some are boys and girls.

Some are grannies and grandads.

But here? Well, here we're all the same. We know each others' stories. We see how our lives all together make up one big endless tale down through the years. All those people who stayed apart for whatever reason, the ones who fought against each other ... they're all here together now.

You remember the spies who the IRA killed the morning I was shot? Well there's a few of them buried here. So is Michael Collins, the fella who arranged the whole thing for the IRA.

And there's us, the people killed in Croke Park, a small handful of souls in a field of thousands. And I was never on my own. My granny and grandad were already buried here.

A year and a half after Bloody Sunday, in July 1922, my uncle Edward was walking home from work with a friend. They lived close enough to each other on Grenville Street, not a million miles from Croke Park.

Well, by that time, Britain had left Ireland, but kept six counties in the north that became Northern Ireland. That caused a civil war in Ireland straight away.

So the lads are walking home and ... can you believe this? Someone shot at them on the street. The one bullet killed the pair of them. My uncle Edward was only fifteen. I wasn't dead two years. The sadness and the shock of it all again ... ah, it was awful.

But people kept going. The living have no choice but to keep going.

The other boys, Jerome and Billy? They're across the way, in another part of the cemetery. For years, some of the people who died on Bloody Sunday had no gravestones, and no one but our families knew where we were.

That might sound cruel, but there were good reasons. Some families couldn't afford a headstone. And a lot of people were frightened that if they did put up a headstone, the police or the soldiers would knock it down again, because we died on Bloody Sunday in Croke Park.

But the years went on and on and family members died. There wasn't as many people around to remember us and where we were buried. This place is huge, like.

I know the stories of the two other lads as well. Like I say, all those lives flow through everyone here. We know each other, even though most of us buried here never met.

Billy Scott's grandad John lived on at home in Fitzroy Avenue till he was eighty-five, when his heart finally gave out. Billy's poor da caught tuberculosis, or TB, a few years later, a terrible disease that took a lot of people before their time. He died in 1925, not five years after Billy. He was only forty-three.

His sister Kathleen died of TB as well, in 1934. She was nineteen. Billy's ma was working then at Jameson's whiskey distillery, and she lived on till she was seventy-seven.

And his brother Fred? Well, Fred married Daisy and they lived in the house on Fitzroy Avenue. He worked away at Jameson's like his ma and died in 1994, when he was eighty-eight. Daisy stayed in Fitzroy Avenue and lived till 2005 and kept the house almost like it was back in Billy's day. After a century living on that small road by Croke Park, she was the last of the Scotts.

After we were all killed, our stories were locked away by the authorities and forgotten down the years. Our names got lost in the telling of Bloody Sunday, which seems odd, but that's what happens sometimes.

But the city can bring us back to life, if you know where to look. If you walk to Little Britain Street, you'll see the old Halston Street church, where me and my uncle William were brought after we died. The fruit market is still there, although it looks a bit different now.

Come to my grave and you'll see that Tom Ryan is buried near me. He was killed in Croke Park too – he was whispering a prayer into the ear of the Tipperary player Michael Hogan when he got shot.

Stand here and you might see in your mind's eye the few people dotted around our graves back in those days when they came to say goodbye. Look to the great green field behind you and think that Michael Feery, another man killed in Croke Park that day, is buried out there somewhere, in a grave with many others.

We are here in this place, but you will see us in Croke Park too, when the game is on. The feeling there is the same as it was when we went to the match. The same thrill rippled through us when the crowd cheered as the teams came out, and the great rising roar when the game started.

Sometimes, if I'm feeling lonely or sad, I let that glorious sunny day take me away by the hand, far away from the end that found me at the bottom of that tree. That Sunday afternoon was my time. That was my day. And I still have it now at the end of all things, that feeling of being so alive.

THE AFTERMATH

• The shooting by members of the RIC, Black and Tans and Auxiliary forces at Croke Park on Bloody Sunday lasted 90 seconds and claimed 14 lives.

• A total of 32 people were killed on Bloody Sunday – 15 alleged spies and agents were killed or mortally wounded by the IRA; three men, Conor Clune and IRA volunteers Dick McKee and Peadar Clancy, died in police custody at Dublin Castle.

• Two courts of military inquiry were held by the British authorities to investigate the events of Bloody Sunday. They both concluded that the police reaction had been 'carried out without orders and was in excess of what was necessitated by the situation', but also that the first shots were fired from within Croke Park, by 'civilians unknown'.

• Newspaper reports, eyewitness accounts, other testimony given by witnesses immediately afterwards and contradictions in the evidence given to both inquiries cast grave doubts over that conclusion.

• Once completed, both inquiries and all evidence was sealed until 1999.

• Over 3,400 people were killed during the Irish War of Independence between January 1919 and July 1921, including 200 civilians. In December 1921, a treaty was signed between Britain and Ireland. This created the 26-county Irish Free State, while six northern counties remained within the United Kingdom as Northern Ireland. There are no reliable figures for the number of people killed in the resulting Civil War in Ireland, which lasted until April 1924.

• In 1926, the stand on the western side of Croke Park was named the Hogan Stand, after Michael Hogan, the Tipperary footballer killed during the shooting.

• Eight of the 14 victims remained in unmarked graves for nearly a century, including Jerome O'Leary and John William Scott. The Gaelic Athletic Association's Bloody Sunday Graves Project continues to erect gravestones to remember the dead.

LIST OF THE BLOODY SUNDAY
DEAD AT CROKE PARK

JANE BOYLE Aged 29, from Lennox Street, Dublin. Jane worked in a butcher's shop. She attended the game with her fiancé Daniel Byron, but was shot and then trampled by the stampeding crowd. Due to be married the following week, Jane was buried in her wedding dress.

JAMES BURKE, 44, from Windy Arbour, Dublin. James worked for the Terenure Laundry. He was killed in a crush near a gate between the modern-day Hill 16 and the Cusack Stand as the crowd tried to escape.

DANIEL CARROLL, 31, from Templederry, Tipperary. Daniel worked as a bar manager and only decided at the last minute to attend the game, having called in to work on his day off. He was shot in the leg after the shooting had ended as he walked away from the ground. 'Wasn't it misfortunate that I went?' he told his boss the following day. He died on the Tuesday.

MICHAEL FEERY, 40, from Gardiner Place, Dublin. A former British soldier, Michael suffered a terrible thigh wound. His died in his army fatigues, his body left unclaimed in hospital for days.

MICHAEL HOGAN, 24, was a farmer from Grangemockler. He played right-corner-back for Tipperary, in his second year on the team. Shot as he crawled to the fence on the park's east side, he died on the field. He is immortalised in the name of the Hogan Stand in Croke Park.

TOM HOGAN, 19, was from Tankardstown, County Limerick, and worked as a mechanic in Dublin. He was shot in the shoulder, which necessitated the amputation of his arm. He died the following Friday, becoming the final victim of the shootings in Croke Park.

JAMES MATHEWS, 38, was a labourer from North Cumberland Street, Dublin. He went to the game with a friend, who escaped. James was shot climbing a wall to safety. His youngest daughter Nancy lived to see a gravestone erected for her father in 2016.

PATRICK O'DOWD, 57, was a labourer from Buckingham Street, Dublin. Originally from Boyerstown, County Meath, he was shot while on top of a wall at the Cusack Stand side, pulling people to safety. Patrick was one of eight victims that lay in an unmarked grave for nearly 100 years.

JEROME O'LEARY, 10, was from Blessington Street, Dublin. Jerome, or Jerry, was helped above the crowd onto a wall at the back of the Canal goal before the game. He was shot in the head as he looked towards the police firing from the canal bridge outside. He was the second victim of the shooting.

WILLIAM ROBINSON, 11, was from Little Britain Street, Dublin. Sitting in a tree at the corner of the modern Davin/ Hogan stands, he turned back as he heard the armoured cars arriving on the bridge behind him. The first victim, William was shot through the chest and shoulder.

TOM RYAN, 27, was from Viking Road, Stoneybatter, Dublin. Originally from Glenbrien in Wexford, Tom worked for a gas company. He was shot as he whispered a prayer into the dying Michael Hogan's ear. An IRA volunteer, he was part of a group involved in the attacks on alleged spies that morning. Their target wasn't at home.

JOHN WILLIAM SCOTT, 14, was from Fitzroy Avenue. Born and reared with Croke Park at the end of his street, Billy was struck by a ricocheted bullet, his chest wound so bad it was thought he had been bayoneted by a soldier.

JAMES TEEHAN, 26, was originally from Gurteen, County Tipperary. He owned a pub on Green Street, Dublin, with his brother John. James was crushed at the same gate as James Burke.

JOSEPH TRAYNOR, 20, was from Ballymount, Dublin. He had cycled to the game with a friend and was shot twice in the back as he tried to escape over the wall at the Canal End. Carried by members of the Ring family to their home at nearby Sackville Gardens, he died shortly after arriving in hospital.

A WORD FROM THE AUTHOR

Is this story true?

Yes it is. Billy, Perry and Jerry are all real boys who lived in 1920 and went to Croke Park to watch a game of football. Their stories at the game and what happened in the aftermath are all real. Their parents and relatives are all real. And the stories and accounts of what happened to them are all real, too.

But what about the conversations and scenes in the boys' homes?

To help tell the story of their lives in a way that makes sense to us, some scenes and conversations had to be imagined and some episodes were created – like the scenes in their homes, Jerry's dad going to Dublin Castle or the adventure involving Perry's friends at the beginning of the book. Charlie Daly was a real person who went to the match with Billy Scott and lived on Clare Road, but his conversation with the student is imagined to help explain the story of Bloody Sunday to us and how the day impacted on the people who survived.

ACKNOWLEDGEMENTS

Thanks to the families of the Bloody Sunday dead for many years of support and patience, and for their remarkable generosity in helping regather and curate the stories of those lost on 21 November 1920. Special thanks to Karina Leeson, great-grandniece of William Robinson, for her help in making this book.

Thanks to Conor Dodd at Glasnevin Cemetery for sharing his amazing research to shed more light on the stories of those who perished and their families. Thanks to all in the GAA who worked tirelessly on various projects over recent years, but especially Cian Murphy, whose endless passion for this story and care for those lost has fuelled so many projects. Thanks to everyone at the GAA Museum, particularly Julianne McKeigue for her support and assistance for this book and beyond. It is truly treasured.

Thanks to David Sweeney for his brilliant illustrations, and to Jon Berkeley for the fantastic cover image. Thanks to O'Brien Press, to Íde Ní Laoghaire and Eoin O'Brien for their work as editors, Emma Byrne for the design and the entire team for bringing this book to fruition. Special thanks to the late Michael O'Brien who coaxed this book into being and offered the most generous and inspirational encouragement throughout its writing.

Thanks to my family, to my late father and my mother who provided the love and support that allowed me to pursue these dreams of mine. To my brother Andrew, whose astounding work on The Bloodied Field podcast transformed the original book into a soundscape that opened the story up for so many people. And to Karen, Thomas, Liam, Adam and Eoin for being my constant inspiration, encouragement and guiding lights.

Our constant hope through the years was merely to regain and protect the memory of the Bloody Sunday dead. We hope we have paid them proper tribute. We are them. They are us. We remember them now and always.